# The
# courtesan's
# Daughter

# also by priscilla galloway

*Snake Dreamer*

*Truly Grim Tales*

ADAPTED FOR YOUNGER READERS:

*Emily of New Moon* by L. M. Montgomery

a novel by
# priscilla galloway

# The courtesan's Daughter

DELACORTE PRESS

Published by
Delacorte Press
an imprint of
Random House Children's Books
a division of Random House, Inc.
1540 Broadway
New York, New York 10036

Visit us on the Web! www.randomhouse.com/teens
Educators and librarians, for a variety of teaching tools, visit us at
www.randomhouse.com/teachers

Library of Congress Cataloging-in-Publication Data

Galloway, Priscilla.
The courtesan's daughter / Priscilla Galloway.
p. cm.
Summary: From humble beginnings, Phano rises to become one of ancient
Athens' most powerful citizens through her marriage to Theo, but they both have
powerful enemies who don't share their political views.
ISBN 0-385-72907-3 (trade)—ISBN 0-385-90052-X (lib. bdg.)
[1. Family life—Greece—Fiction. 2. Greece—Politics and government—To 146
B.C.—Fiction. 3. Greece—History—Macedonian Expansion, 359-323 B.C.—
Fiction. 4. Courtesans—Greece—Athens—Fiction.] I. Title.
PZ7.G1385 Co 2002
[Fic]—dc21
2002001496

The text of this book is set in 11.5-point Electra.

Book design by Angela Carlino

Printed in the United States of America

October 2002

10 9 8 7 6 5 4 3 2 1

BVG

*To my loving husband, Howard Collum,
who has shared my companionship
during the past four years with the
characters in this book*

*Small opportunities are often the beginning of great enterprises.*
                                    — DEMOSTHENES

*Children believe everything that happens is somehow their fault, but they also believe in happy endings, despite all evidence to the contrary.*
          — MARGARET ATWOOD, *The Blind Assassin*

# one

## Ancient Athens, 350 B.C.E.

"Gate, ho!"

"Minta, see who's making that racket," Mama commanded. "Don't unbar the door unless you're sure of him."

"I'll go too, Mama." I put out a hand to stop my spindle. We were safe in my father's house in Athens, the little house by the Whispering Herm; nobody could touch us here. My heart thudded nonetheless.

I lifted my grandmother's thigh shield with both hands and set it very carefully on the floor. Then I ran. Minta is a faithful slave, but she has no judgment about men. Anyone with a laugh and an easy word can get by her. By the time I reached the gate room, the fool had already lifted the heavy bar. Two men pushed past her. I didn't recognize the first one, but I knew Phrynion at once, squatty frog-face, with his bulging eyes and fat, red pouty lips. He looked up at me and laughed. My hatred surged back as I heard the nasty sound. His right hand still tugged at his scraggly beard. His teeth were still yellow and his breath still stank of garlic and decay. After three years of freedom, Phrynion had me in his power again. My nightmare had come true.

❊

I closed my eyes and felt as if I were nine again, and not almost fourteen years old. I remembered the child I had been, and the desperate year whose memories were distilled into my ghastly dreams.

It all began with another of Father's get-rich-quick schemes. These schemes always demanded money, which Father always failed to have. None of his friends and relatives would lend him so much as a copper obol, so he was delighted to make an arrangement with one of the city officials, even at a very high interest rate.

Unfortunately, the official had "borrowed" from the public treasury. When arrested, he pleaded for mercy. He said Father had blackmailed him. This scheme not only failed to make us rich; Father had to leave Athens in a hurry, without Mama and me.

The rent for our little rooms behind the cobbler's shop was paid ahead for one month. If Mama didn't find another place, we'd be out on the street. No use asking Father's people; they might despise him, but they hated her. I didn't see that clearly at the time, of course. If I had been older, I'd have been terrified. Maybe not, though. Mama inspired perfect confidence. I never doubted that she would turn this seeming calamity to our advantage. She could not solve Father's problems, but she would look after us.

Mama had lived with Phrynion long ago. He promised to give her slaves, fine clothes and parties if she came back to him again. "Just until your father sends for us," she told me. "You'll like it, Phano—a big house, and meat on the table every day. I can manage Phrynion well enough. I have done it before."

Mama was wrong, and we all paid for it. This time Phrynion did the managing. Minta slept with the slaves. I slept with the pigs. Mama slept with Phrynion. He barred her door whenever he went out. He beat me every time he saw the hatred in my eyes.

Like most rich men's homes, Phrynion's house was built around an inner courtyard. It was two stories high, with a set of stairs on each side of the courtyard leading to the balcony and across it to the upper rooms. The pigsty was on the ground floor at the far end, as far as possible from the gatehouse, where Nesso was always on guard. As winter wore on, I came to believe that my only escape would be through death. Often enough, I hoped it would be soon.

The only good thing in that desperate year was that I

learned to spin. Delia, the housekeeper, taught me, but I have a natural skill for the work. The great goddess Athene gave me the gift. When I sat, or stood, with spindle twirling, my back no longer ached from Phrynion's beatings. Indeed, the hated house itself vanished. I passed into some dream where nothing existed but the spinner, the wool basket and the fine yarn twirling from my hands.

Mama seldom saw me, but she did manage an hour or so on my tenth birthday, which otherwise went without celebration. She gave me a wooden box, as black as my hair, so highly polished that I could see my dark reflection in its lid. Inside, wrapped in a fine shawl, was a clay shield made to protect a spinner's thigh when she sat at her work. "This was passed down in your mother's family," Mama told me. "Take good care of it." I would have slept with it, if it had not been safer with my wool.

Phrynion seized my first work, the blanket I had spun and woven to keep myself from another winter of trying to cuddle up to a stinky old sow so I would not freeze to death. If a child's curses could kill, Phrynion would have died in that hour.

At last Mama succeeded in a scheme of her own. She planted the idea in the greedy man's head that his brothers were plotting to inherit all their mother's property when she died. As the idea took hold, Phrynion's anxiety grew. He knew his brothers only too well. As soon as the spring rains ended, he gave careful instructions to Nesso, the gatekeeper, then set out to pay a filial visit to his family's country home. Delia went with him to visit her relatives there.

Minta unbarred Mama's door.

If Phrynion had come back and caught us, he would have beaten Minta to death. When a slave disobeyed her master, he could do that. Minta belonged to Mama, but that would not have made any difference. We packed with sweaty fingers.

"We have three days," Mama told us. "We have to get away, far enough so that Phrynion won't follow. We have to confuse him, so he can't figure out where we've gone."

"Where *are* we going?" I asked. "How will Father find us, if it's far away?"

"Better worry how Phrynion *won't* find us," Mama snapped. "Stephanos could be dead, who knows?"

I howled at that, and Minta hugged me, sobbing as well. Mama's arms went round the two of us. "Very well," she said. "Minta, go to the shop where we used to live. Tell the cobbler—the master, nobody else, mind you—the message for Stephanos is Megara. Megara, that's all." She tugged at the ring on her little finger, her gold and ivory ring with a picture of two geese leading a chariot and a woman driving. Mama loved that ring, and so did I. I knew what she was going to do before she opened her mouth.

"Do you have to give it away?"

Mama glared at me. "Minta," she said, "give this ring—this ring—to the cobbler. Ask him not to sell it for three years. If Stephanos comes, he'll buy it back and pay extra, but only after he finds us—in Megara—and we're safe." She gave me her exasperated look; then she shoved the ring back on her hand.

5

"No, Minta," she said. "Don't go. Phrynion knows we lived behind the cobbler's shop. He'll look for us there; he'll do all he can to sniff our track. What if he caught us because we left a message for Stephanos? Well, Phano? If nobody knows where we are, Phrynion can't find out. Don't look like you've lost your last friend, girl. In a year, Phrynion will have other things on his mind. Time enough then to send word to Athens. If your father has to wait a few months, that's no matter. We have waited for news from him, haven't we?"

Mama was right. She usually is. Minta had something to say, though. "Mistress, may I speak?" she asked. Mama gestured impatiently, and Minta continued. "Whatever we tell the cobbler, Phrynion will find out. Is that right?"

"Of course he will. Can't you see it? Phrynion sends a thug with a few pieces of silver. The thug gives our former landlord the gift, asks about us, promises to send the household's sandals to his shop for repair—plenty of work now, and for years to come—then looks around and wonders if the shop is safe from fire. I can almost hear him. Bribery and a threat, nothing you can take to the authorities, but the cobbler isn't a fool, he'll get the message. So? What's in your mind?"

Minta hurried on. "Do like you said, the message, the ring—but say you've gone back to Corinth," she said. "Phrynion will believe that, won't he? By the time he knows different, we'll be clear away."

A slow grin crinkled Mama's mouth. "That's brilliant, Minta," she said, "more than you know. The cobbler will believe it. Phrynion will believe it. But Stephanos, if he comes back and hears that message, he *won't* believe it. When I bought my freedom, I promised never to go back to Corinth. Phrynion doesn't know that, but Stephanos does."

Mama found several more ways to cover our tracks, but we had a worrisome time on the road. Perhaps it was a mistake to take so much of Phrynion's furniture with us, as well as the smaller jars of wine and precious olive oil from his storage room, and Obole, who had been Phrynion's slave before he gave her to Mama. "It's not stealing," Mama said. "Phrynion promised me much more than this."

Minta and I did not point out the obvious: without the heavy load, we could have moved twice as fast. Dusty and exhausted, we came to Megara at last. I was right to have confidence in Mama. We did not become rich, but we ate well, better than any time I could recall. When a year had passed, Mama sent a message to Athens. She made a kind of treasure hunt of it, full of secret clues. When she had finished dictating, the scribe handed the wax tablet to her and said he had never transcribed a stranger letter. I couldn't understand it much better than he could. If father saw it, would it make sense to him?

It must have made sense, because the day came that brought him to our door. He was dirty from the road, and smelled strongly of horse, but Mama ran as fast as I did to throw her arms around him. We had had no news of him for more than two years. Now, all his news was good. His father had died and left him the little house. His family had used their influence to have the blackmail charges against him dropped.

"For the good of the family name," Father explained wryly. A powerful family can help poor relatives in many ways, even if they are not generous with money. Whatever their motive, I was thankful. I did not blame our relations for our money troubles; Father had never repaid them in the past.

Mama sold her business in Megara and we came home. No Athenian can be totally happy anywhere else. Father and I stood on top of the great hill of the Acropolis and breathed the pure air, in and out. We laid our sacrifices at the feet of Athene. Father cut off a lock of his dark hair. I gave my finest weaving, a hanging of green-gray olive trees.

Alas, our rejoicing was short-lived. Our beloved Athens suffers under a new threat, the most dangerous we have ever faced. Father says so, and it is impossible to doubt, though I wish he did not talk about it all the time. Mama pats him on the shoulder and looks interested. I can't tell if she is pretending or not.

The threat comes from Philip of Macedon in the north. Athenians are bitterly divided about what is best to do. Father and his friends say Philip will conquer Athens and the whole of Attica if we don't arm ourselves, rebuild our navy and fortify our walls. Other people say that ships, walls and armor would be a waste of good money; we Athenians are good with words, we should negotiate with

Philip. Both groups refuse to compromise; arguments often turn into fights in the meeting place or in the streets.

Mama and I have lived quietly at home since our return. If we ventured out, we walked with our shawls pulled around our faces. Even then, we stayed in the neighborhood. The more time that went by before Phrynion heard we were back, the less angry he would be. A person can't be looking over her shoulder all the time, however. Sometimes lately we have forgotten to be afraid. Today Minta opened the door.

Looking down at Frog-face, I was afraid again. Phrynion was staring at me. My tunic is modest, but those bulging eyes wanted to bore holes through the fine wool right to my skin. He's short enough; it's easy for him to look where he wants.

Oh, Minta, how could you be such a fool?

# two

"Phano! Look at your master when he speaks to you."

I hoped for a crazy moment that I was in my own bed and would wake from this nightmare, but I knew that the hateful voice was real, that Phrynion had invaded our home, that Minta and I were already his prisoners and that Mama would soon be seized as well. We had no courtyard, no gatehouse and no strong slave at the entrance to keep us safe.

Phrynion looked at me, his tongue moving slowly in and out between his fat red lips, the frog looking at the fly, thinking of dinner. What if I could never go up to my loft again? Would somebody tidy my yarn away? Would somebody wrap my beloved thigh shield in flannel and set it in its dark chest? Would somebody stand at my loom and finish weaving my purple cloak?

Little, stupid, nasty man, Phrynion fed on my fear. He loved it. Rage swelled my body. I faced him, hands clenched under my flowing sleeves.

"Phano, little Phano, not so little anymore." His voice was smooth as oil from the first pressing. I wanted to stop my ears, but my hands didn't move. "What a pleasure to see you again. More than three years, isn't it? You've put on your woman's girdle. Hmmm, I wonder if I will give myself the pleasure of untying it, or if I'll sell you to one of my friends."

"No."

"Is that the best you can do? 'No,'" he mimicked. "Where's that cheating mother of yours? Stop hiding, Nera! Minta is here, that's good. Where are my other slaves?"

"Minta is not your slave," I told him. Thanks to Mother Hera, we had sold Obole into a good home before we left Megara. The very idea of living in the same city as Phrynion was enough to make her burn the oatcakes or drop the wine pitcher. Nesso the gatekeeper vanished when he learned we were going back. He had run away from Phrynion; he also ran away from us. Minta might know where he had gone, but I did not.

"Where are the others?" Phrynion demanded.

I tried to sound brave. "Where you'll never get them."

"You won't get us either, you piece of cow dung," snorted Mama. She swept down the stairs. I relaxed a

11

little. Mama is a presence, there's no denying. Sooner or later, things tend to happen the way she wants. Often, I hate what she does, but I thank the gods—and Mama— for the results. Mama makes me very mixed up.

Now she bristled all over. Her big eyes looked black, and her face was scarlet, almost as red as her hair. Her right hand was hidden in the folds of her chiton, likely gripping her small bronze knife. Mama's chiton was pinned on the right shoulder with a huge ancient brooch in the likeness of Hippolyta, the Amazon queen. The brooch pin was Hippolyta's bronze spear.

For three hundred years, women of Athens have been forbidden to wear brooch pins long and strong enough to kill a man. Phrynion should have been scared. As far as I could tell, however, he was only angry. Like Mama. Why not? They both had reason.

Mama's eyes raked Phrynion. "I am a free woman," she spat. "No one knows it better than you. Get out of here before my husband comes home, and take your bully boy with you." She swiveled toward the man who still held Minta, and slapped his face.

This was a mistake. Phrynion shouted, and two more men pushed through our open door. Before we could do anything, the bullies hustled the three of us into the street.

"Kleeta!" Mama screamed. Our neighbor opened her upstairs shutter. Kleeta did not approve of our household, but Mama always took the trouble to charm anyone in sight, in case she needed help, and our neighbor was no exception. "Tell my husband that Phrynion has kidnapped us."

"Tell him what you like, lady," Phrynion laughed. "I don't know what these liars have told you. I'm just taking back my property, and I'll lash them until they bleed. These slaves won't run away again."

"Kleeta, you know us, we're free women, he's the liar," Mama shouted again. "Send for Stephanos, he's in the agora. Tell the judge!"

Phrynion slapped Mama's mouth. In a moment, bright blood began to run down her chin. The men jostled us along. Mama dragged her feet, but Minta put up no resistance at all. Indeed, soon she was sneaking little smiles at the men who held her. Where was her loyalty?

I felt nothing but cold despair. Why had I thought Mama and I were free of Phrynion? Father had promised to protect us when we left Megara and returned to Athens. Could he? Phrynion was rich. Father had no property except the little house. Mama had run away from Phrynion twice, the first time before I was born. Now, he had us again. He would whip her, and me, as if we were really slaves. This time we would not be able to run away.

*I am a free woman of Athens*, I told myself, over and over. *I am almost fourteen years old. I am not a slave to be whipped, or sold, and only the man I marry will untie my girdle on our wedding night.* I lifted my head and pulled my scarf around my face, so that I could see without being exposed to every man's stare. Phrynion watched and laughed, as if he could read my thoughts.

A fine drizzle dampened our clothes and chilled our skin. Our captors hustled us through the muddy streets.

All too soon we came to the outer wall of Phrynion's house. My foot touched the cold marble floor of the gate-house. As I dragged along behind Mama, I felt as if I had never been away. I felt dizzy and sick; then I felt nothing at all.

❀

"Where are your wits, Phano?" Mama's sharp voice brought me back to the present. An acrid smell filled my nostrils, somebody burning a feather under my nose. I sneezed violently and sat up. I knew at once where we were, in the women's quarters, upstairs in Phrynion's house. I stood up and walked unsteadily to the door. I lifted the latch and pulled, but the door did not move. Phrynion or his men could get in, but we could not get out that way.

I turned away violently. "That stupid Minta, this is all her fault. Doesn't a slave ever stop to think? She opened our front door—and then she laughed and made eyes at those beasts who kidnapped us. Opening the door was stupid. Laughing with our enemies is treacherous. She needs a good whipping, Mama. I'd gladly beat her myself."

"She would want you to draw blood," said Mama. "She did open the door. Poor Minta, her shoulders are heavy with guilt."

"Not so anyone could notice," I said.

"That's true," Mama replied. "She hides it, Phano. You don't have to believe me, but it's the truth. She has as much to lose in this as any of us. Forget about whipping her. Save your strength to fight our enemies."

"You know how to suck the anger out of me, Mama," I said. "I don't know how you do it. You are right about saving our strength to fight Phrynion. I'll see how I feel about Minta after we're free. Where is she? Why isn't she here with us?"

Mama shrugged. "She is making friends with the bully boys, I hope. Being practical. She'll turn up. There's a guard on the stairs, but it will soon be dark. Can you still climb down from the balcony, Phano?"

"Maybe." The wide corridor ran the full square of the house, overlooking the courtyard. I smiled at the ancient olive tree in the nearby corner. It had been my ladder often enough when I was nine. It wouldn't be so easy now; I was heavier, and my long tunic would get in the way.

"If I can get down, I'll look for Minta," I said slowly. "Maybe the kitchen slaves will give me a bowl of lentils. We can't hope for more, there was never any food to spare from that kitchen."

"You must talk to the gateman, Phano, smile at him, sideways, dropping your eyelids—let me see you do it."

Mama had been teaching me these tricks forever, though she knew I hated them. Now she frowned and stamped her dainty foot. "Who'd believe it? I have brought you up, I, Nera, the most famous courtesan in Corinth, yet you have no woman's guile. Again, girl—like this!" Mama batted her pretty eyes at me and smiled her most mischievous smile. In spite of myself, I smiled back.

"That's better. Now, what can we ask that he may be willing to do?"

"Do you need a doctor, Mama?"

"That's it! I don't, but you do, and right away. The healer near the water fountain, in the street of potters."

My clothes were tucked up and both legs were over the balcony railing when the door behind me opened and I heard Minta's voice. The nearest branch of the olive seemed small and very far away. I wanted to be brave, but truly I was frightened to trust myself to the tree and even more frightened to talk to the gateman, not so much because he was bent and gnarled even more than the tree as because he would likely yell for his master as soon as I appeared. Then Phrynion would have me in his power indeed, and might not wait to sell me to one of his friends. I swung my legs back over the railing faster than I had swung them out in the first place, then loosened the cord at my waist and rearranged my tunic.

"Phano!" Mama called. "Your message again, Minta."

"The master bids us all to dine with him and his friends this evening, Mistress. He commands, pardon, he asks us to play and sing for them, perhaps to dance. Please, Mistress, meat is roasting on the spit, and the wine jugs are full. Whatever follows, we will face it better after a good meal."

"Phrynion is not my master, Minta. What if we refuse this invitation?" Mama's voice was icy.

"If you do not obey him, beg pardon, if you and Mistress Phano do not dine with his guests and entertain them, he promises to whip me until I bleed. He did not say what he would do to you. Please, Mistress, they are only men, after all. It would be easier to do what he asks."

"Spoken like a true slave."

Color flared into Minta's white face. Mama laughed. "Phrynion has no right to whip you, though that would hardly stop him." Mama's eyes flickered in my direction. "I'm not a fool, Minta. I'll dine with Phrynion and his fellow thugs. 'Know your enemy,' that's my motto. Maybe one of them will agree to tell Stephanos where we are.

"You and I will accept Phrynion's kind invitation. His meat is as good as another man's. However, Phano is indisposed. I fear a fever. Phano must sit with the household servants by the kitchen fire tonight. Come, I'll tell Phrynion myself."

I followed Mama and Minta down the stairs into the courtyard. Mama led us to the kitchen. Delia sat by the fire, her old spindle in her hand.

"Keep Phano with you all night," said Mama. "I'll reward you, Delia, you may be sure. Say what you must—fever?—red spots on her back?—anything, but don't let the girl out of your sight. Agreed?"

"I'll do what I can," said Delia. "I had a daughter once." She shrugged. I took up another spindle and a basket of loose wool and sat on the bench beside her. I did not say anything; nor did she. Under our hands, clumps of wool turned into fine, even yarn.

Two slaves turned three chickens, a goose and two great haunches of beef on the spits; juice sizzled on the fire. One of the slaves slashed off a thick wedge of meat from the underside, where it wouldn't show, and left it for us. He winked at me as he left the kitchen, his muscles straining with the weight of the huge silver platter. I'd never thought I would feel hungry, but the glorious smell was irresistible. Mama was right, Phrynion's meat was as good as another man's.

Delia and I listened to the noise from the andron, voices and laughter. Wine jugs came and went, and the voices grew louder, Mama's as loud as any of them. Somebody tuned the strings of a lyre: Mama, I knew her touch. I knew the song as well, a vulgar ditty about a sailor with a different wife in every port. Mama never sings it unless she has drunk more wine than she should. I blushed, thankful she was too far away for Delia to hear all the words.

My eyelids drooped. I nearly fell off the bench, and was about ready to lay my cloak on the floor and try to sleep when Minta appeared in the doorway. A man had his arm around her, and the two of them staggered across the room to stand in front of me. Minta tried to talk, but she kept giggling. All I could understand was that she had a message for me from Mama.

"You tell us, Stavros," Delia said at last.

"This girl, her mother wants her."

"At's ri," mumbled Minta.

They wove across the courtyard, heading not to the men's dining room, but to the gate. Father must have come for us. What else could be happening so late at night? I ran ahead of them—right into the arms of one of Phrynion's thugs.

"Help!" I thought my lungs would burst with the scream.

The man slapped my mouth so hard my teeth felt loose. He threw me down on the ground and tied a rope around my ankles, another around my wrists. Then he threw me like a sack of flour into the back of a cart.

The cart was light. I bounced as the horses pulled it along at a smart trot. My right hip was bruised, my right shoulder aching. Where were Mama and Minta?

The driver of the cart was the young bully who had tricked Minta into opening the door of Father's house—only that morning, though already it might have been in another lifetime. His gray cloak was woven of coarse cloth, tied with string: likely he did not possess so much as a brooch.

The man beside the driver wore a cloak of green wool, striped with white and narrow bands of gold, woven from yarn as fine as any I could have spun. It was pinned with a brooch of carved ivory and gold: a rich man, perhaps also a gentleman.

My bound hands tingled, but they had not yet turned numb. I humped myself along the boards, trying to get closer. "Ouch!"

The green cloak shimmered as the rich man turned. "Sliver in your bum, girl? No more than you deserve."

"Please, sir, where are you taking me?"

"That's your master's business, slave, not yours."

My temper gets the better of me too often, Mama says. Pretend it's a play, she says; pretend you're on the stage at the Festival of Dionysos. No matter that no woman will ever play on that stage. Indeed, says Mama, we play on the stage of life! Fine words! But he called me a slave, and that is not in the play of my life if I can help it. Gentleman or not, I spat at his lying face. I got more spit on myself than on him, and couldn't wipe it off, which made me angrier still.

"Don't you dare call me a slave," I hissed. "I am a free woman, like Mama."

"Liar."

I brought up both my legs and kicked at him. He dodged easily, looking down at me with contempt. I felt some contempt for myself, actually. The power of my kick sent me down on my back on the bare wood of the cart, exposing my legs in a fashion not at all suitable for a proper Athenian woman, which I try so hard to be.

The man shrugged, then turned his back on me again. Mama would have talked to him. She would have looked at him as if nobody else existed in the world. In five minutes, he would have been telling her the story of his life. In an hour, he would have been telling her his family secrets and giving her a precious pendant or earrings.

A light rain was still falling. My cloak lay on the kitchen floor at Phrynion's house. I wore only the fine tunic I had put on early that morning. I shivered. My teeth began to knock against each other. The man looked at me and made a face. He unpinned his cloak, then pinned it again.

"Give me the reins," he told the man beside him. "Throw your cloak over that baggage behind us."

"My cloak?"

"No doubt you're both full of fleas, so do it. Hurry up, man, Phrynion won't thank us if she dies of a fever. His money would be gone out the window."

What did that mean? I couldn't make sense of it. In a moment, however, the rough cloak fell around me, covering even my face. Sleep would have been the last thing I expected, but warmth spread through my body and the jolting cart became a kind of rocking cradle. I blinked a time or two and closed my eyes.

The next thing I heard was Phrynion's hateful voice. "Come down, Phano. This is your master calling. Come down—or don't come down, and I'll come up. Just you and me, that's what you'd like, isn't it?"

Nothing could have got me moving faster. I sat up and banged my head. Dim light from an unshuttered window showed a wooden beam. Above me, a low roof sloped up to a ridge. "I'm coming down."

My bare feet picked up slivers from the rough floor as I ran to the opening where a ladder poked through. Three men stared up at me: Phrynion and the two men from the cart.

"Where is Mama? Where am I? What's happening?" My voice sounded scared, even to me. Shameful. Disgusting Phrynion, making me ashamed of myself.

"I'm taking back my own, girl. You know what your mother stole from me. I'm taking it back. So every minute

you don't come down, it's another blow with my whip."
Phrynion had a bald patch on the top of his head, a big
circle shining up at me. I would have liked to laugh at
him.

"Come now, she's young, give her a minute or two." I
looked down gratefully at the younger man before climbing down the ladder to look up at him.

"Where am I?"

The young man answered me. "This is my family
farm. Your mother—I'm afraid we had to lock her up."

"By the gods, she won't get out in a hurry!" Phrynion's
hand went to his face.

"Scratched you, didn't she?" The third man, the thug,
laughed.

Phrynion swelled up like the toad he so much resem-
bled. "She won't be so feisty after a day without food or
water. She won't be so mouthy when I've finished with
*you*." He leered at me. "So, do I take you myself, or sell
you to my friend? Or both? You've been eyeing her, Theo.
Her mother's a wildcat, but this one's tame enough. What
do you offer?" He laughed. "Come, man, make it worth
my while."

"If you take me by force, you or any other man, you
will answer to my father and to the laws of Athens."

"Brave words, even if your voice is shaking," said
Theo. He seemed puzzled. "What does it matter to you,
girl?" he asked. "Don't pretend you're a virgin still!"

"I am a virgin." Phrynion turned to me, hand raised,
but he was half a dozen steps away. I had time for a few

words. "I have made my vow to Artemis to kill myself if any man but my husband unties my girdle and takes my maidenhead."

"A slave girl! Come, now!" But he sounded shaken, enough to give me courage. Phrynion's fist knocked me to the ground, but he had sent the blow to my stomach, not my face. Phrynion always hit me where it wouldn't show. Lucky for me he remembered he didn't want to knock out my teeth!

I looked up at Theo, gulping for breath. "Not slave. Free. Told you. Stephanos—see him, see records."

Phrynion too breathed raggedly. His face was patchy red.

Theo looked from me to Phrynion and back again. "Let's take our time on this," he said quietly. "I'll see you right, Phrynion my friend, never fear. You're not well, man, she's put you in a rage. It's lucky we've brought her to my place. My women will take charge of her. Under guard, of course. She won't get away."

"Fifteen minas they cost me, you've seen my receipts."

"I have, that's why I helped you. Well, I can see Stephanos too."

"How does he make his living? By blackmail—never believe anything that man says or trust anything he shows you."

"Maybe—but I've heard much the same about you, Phrynion, and not believed the evil I've heard. Be satisfied, man, you'll get what's right."

I was still lying on the mucky floor, pretending I didn't

exist, and wishing Pluto would come from the underworld to lend me his cap of darkness so that I could disappear. "Get up," said Theo briskly. "Follow me, and don't make trouble, you hear?"

"Yes, sir." Mama would have been pleased, if she could have heard. Truly, though, I felt as meek as I sounded.

The housekeeper made me carry washing water from the courtyard well to fill two great tubs, one for me, the other for my clothes. "Who did you steal this from?" she grunted when she looked at my tunic.

"I made it." I gave her stare back again. "Give me a spindle and I'll show you, after I'm clean."

So I spent the rest of my second day as a captive in a way I had not expected, in the women's quarters of a re-spectable house, with a spindle and yarn in my hands. It may seem heartless, but if I thought of Mama now and then, I did nothing to help her. If Mama thought she could charm Phrynion this time, she was mistaken. Theo, perhaps. I choked on the thought. Then I gave my atten-tion to the wool basket, and the world seemed no longer upside down. If only I could have had my thigh shield! I tried sitting on a four-legged stool, but soon had to stop to rub my aching leg, so I stood to my work and let the spin-dle twirl free.

# three

I heard the clatter of hooves late in the afternoon, and was not surprised when a slave woman came to tell me I was wanted downstairs. Theo looked tired and dusty. Obviously, he had ridden hard and had not stopped to wash. Phrynion stared at him. "Well?" he barked.

Theo moved a stool. He motioned for me to sit down before seating himself. "Fine courtesy, for a slave!" snorted Phrynion.

"That's as may be," replied Theo. "Your case is against Nera and Stephanos, friend Phrynion, not against this girl."

"Daughter of a slave goes to the master, in case you've forgotten."

"Not so simple as that. You didn't tell me the whole story when you asked for my help. It's a matter for negotiation, don't you think? That's what Stephanos wants."

"It's not only the money, how about my furniture? How about my slaves?"

"Nera wronged you, I don't disagree. You should have what belongs to you."

"I keep the women until it's settled."

"You'd be responsible. No touching, no squeezing the merchandise." Theo grinned, one man to another. Disgusting. "It would be expensive too. Why not send them back to Stephanos?"

"I might as well have had them arrested in the first place. Let Stephanos answer in court."

"You wanted to save the cost of courts and lawyers, as I recall. Have you completely changed your mind?"

"Damn the cost." Phrynion spat the words. "All right, Theo, I'll charge her in front of the Polemarch. Stephanos can bail her out. He can keep her while we negotiate. That way, she can't run away again. They pay me what they owe, or she's mine again, and her daughter too. You're a good man, Theo, you can act for me."

"I'll take Nera before the Polemarch, Phrynion. Tomorrow morning, not tonight. It's been a long day. No doubt Stephanos will post a bond for her release. I've given orders for Nera and Minta to be taken to the women's quarters. You'll join them in a few minutes, Phano. Now, Phrynion, I'm afraid you'll have to find another negotiator. I've agreed to act for the other side."

I stopped myself from throwing my arms around Theo, but it was a near thing. Phrynion's red lips moved in and out, like a fish just pulled from the sea. At last he found his voice. "I will not stay for dinner, Theo. I wish you joy of your new friends." At the door he turned and looked at both of us. I've never seen such venom in any human face.

"A poor enough excuse for a friend," said Theo quietly, "but a worse enemy, I fear. Will it offend your respectability, Phano, if I invite myself to dine with the women tonight?"

"A slave's respectability? In your own home? Why should you ask?"

"Don't hold that against me, Phano. I know better now. Give me a chance!" He was pleading with me. I liked it, even if it did make me feel like Mama. Perhaps I have not understood Mama as well as I believed. Mama would have made him beg. It's amazing how much can flash through one's mind, how fast. I am not Mama, to make a man behave like a child.

"Thank you for asking, Theo. Thank you for saving me. You are welcome to dine with us." It was a poor excuse for a speech, but the best I could do. Theo nodded.

"I'll get the grime off, then."

Dinner promised to be a lively meal. Nothing brings Mama to life like a man she does not yet know. Theo was good-looking in a craggy way, tall and gangly. Athenian men wear their hair short and trim their beards. Theo followed that style, but hair and beard were a color I'd never seen before: corn yellow. His hair lay in soft curls against his temples; my hands itched to stroke it. Most people have dark hair, brown or black like mine. Mama brightens hers with henna, but it is naturally dark red; unusual enough, though not unique. I've wished sometimes my hair was that color.

I don't usually wish I had Mama's skills with men, but that night I envied her. Five minutes after Theo sat down, she was beside him on the couch, pouring his wine and plumping up his cushions, giving his neck and shoulders a friendly rub. She made it seem completely natural.

"Have you known Phrynion for a long time?"

"He was my uncle's friend more than mine, until recently." Theo's fair skin reddened. "Politics comes into it."

Mama smiled. "In Athens, politics comes into everything. Tell me more."

"It's hardly of interest to Phano, Nera — and I doubt it's really interesting to you."

"You mistake me, Theo. I was raised on politics. Besides, everything that affects Stephanos interests me. Politics is his life. Phrynion is a miser, a rich man who hates to spend an obol. His political views move in the same direction as everything else in his life. I know him, do I not?"

"Better than I, it seems. Athens is in desperate straits, but he refuses to see it. In my grandfather's day, we controlled the seas. Pericles made our navy the envy of the world. The long walls reached from Piraeus harbor to the city. So long as they stood, we could supply our needs. Athens could never fall to a siege."

"And now? What do you believe?"

Theo shrugged. He spoke bitterly. "What rich man offers to build a new trireme now, and to equip and arm her? Men have stolen stone from the long walls to build their homes, and their tombs. Athens has been at peace too long."

"Did you believe Phrynion would vote for higher taxes to defend Athens? Is that why you helped him? I wonder at you, Theo."

"I was a fool."

I had had enough. "You were not a fool," I said hotly. "Phrynion fooled you once, but you know him now. He fooled my mama twice. Has anyone else done that, Mama?"

"No." Mama spat it out.

"You're no fool, Mama. Theo, you are not a fool either. You want to rebuild the long walls. You want new ships for the navy. Father says the same thing, almost in the same words. That means high taxes for everyone with money, Father says. Do you agree?"

"Do I agree? A political discussion, by Zeus! I've never met a young woman at all like you, Phano. Earlier today, I was ashamed of how I talked to you. I'm still ashamed—I talked as if you knew things you shouldn't know."

"You thought I was a slave. I am a respectable woman, Theo."

Theo's lips twitched. "A very *young* woman, Phano,

but respectable, certainly. You're beautiful as well. I'm supposed to marry Chloe, Phrynion's niece, and she's dull as ditchwater. So is every other Athenian woman of good family I've met. Why are you so different?"

"There!" Mama was delighted. "How many times have I told you, my girl? I have seen to her education, Theo. If Phano should want my kind of life, she is prepared for it."

"A courtesan's education, you mean? I had never thought much about it." Theo blinked.

"How do we hold our own at your dinner parties, Theo? Apollodorus the philosopher taught me rhetoric and grammar. Sappho was my dancing teacher, and Leonidas, of the family of Orpheus, for music and poetry. The greatest artist in Corinth taught me to draw and paint."

"Mama!" My face burned with shame.

"Don't you spit on me, Phano. My business has put food in your mouth and clothes on your back and a roof over your head. You could do worse."

"Thank you for nothing, Mama. You forget your place, the wife of a citizen of Athens."

"I am a wife, but not a model of respectability, Aphrodite be praised."

Smiling broadly, Theo intervened in our argument. "I'm fascinated," he said. "You're a respectable woman, Phano, and interesting as well. What's wrong with that?"

What, indeed? Mama's business did support us in Megara, it's true. Men of all sizes and shapes came to the house. There was a little spy hole in the wall of the andron, and I spent many hours there, hoping to see something interesting. The men sat on couches. Obole and the other girls sat beside them, popping grapes into their mouths, or holding the wine cup to their lips. I used to think that all men turned into babies when they came to our house. Men certainly like to hear themselves talk. I didn't understand most of what they said; it was dull stuff anyway.

Theo was not like that. He wanted Mama to talk. He wanted *me* to talk. Usually I chatter on, saying whatever comes into my head. Now I wanted to impress Theo, and I couldn't think of anything to say. He and Mama settled into talk of politics. For once, I wanted to understand.

"Danger from the north...The threat from Macedon...Philip's great army...The treasury of Athens... Alliance with Thebes?...Empty shipyards and idle shipwrights, and the navy of Athens dependent on rotting ships."

It should have scared me awake, and might have, if I hadn't heard it all so often, for so long. A person becomes numb to talk of horrors eventually, especially if the talk goes on and on but nothing changes. I hid my yawns for a while. At some point, Mama called Minta to take me up to bed.

31

# four

Waiting in the road next morning were high-stepping horses and a fancy cart with cushions and a box tall enough to allow us to hide our faces easily from others passing by. Theo knew how to do a thing in style!

Minta served dates and wine before our journey began. Theo, in his green cloak, led out a chocolate brown gelding. He removed the pit from a date and offered the fruit to the horse, which nibbled it delicately from his outstretched hand. "I sent a messenger to Stephanos last night," Theo told us, "but I'll ride with you myself and see you safe."

Father met us not far from Athens. He strode along the road, looking hot and dusty. The driver gave him a hand up into the cart, where he sank down gratefully onto a cushion beside Mama. Theo tied his horse behind the cart and climbed in as well. "We don't have far to go," he told the driver, "but we need to talk, and I'd rather keep moving while we do it. Take it easy on the horses, poor beasts, with all this added weight to pull.

"How goes it, Stephanos?"

"I have posted bail with the Polemarch already," Father began. "Wife, you can't run away this time, it would cost me my house. Phrynion might have taken my word for it."

"Did you talk to Phrynion yourself?" asked Theo. "Was that wise?"

"It may have made your job more difficult, settling things, though we did not come to blows. I restrained myself. 'Your house is full of my property,' he told me. 'Why would I take your word for anything?'" Father clenched his fists, remembering.

"You did well, keeping your temper," said Mama admiringly. "I would have hit him."

"I almost did. He saw it too. He backed off, the slimy toad. 'Let's not start a brawl,' he whined. 'Let's do what we've agreed.' I had one question for him first. 'Did you protect my daughter's maidenhood?'

"'Whatever she was, she is,' he told me, 'or rather, she *was* when she left my home. If she came here a virgin, she may be a virgin still. I can't answer for anything that may have happened last night, of course.'" Father's fury erupted in a rumbling noise, deep in his throat, the kind of noise that might be made by an angry bear.

I felt the blood hot in my face.

"Daughter?"

"I am safe," I mumbled. I could not tell him what Phrynion had almost done. I felt cheap and dirty, remembering his threats.

Father turned to Mama. "Were the three of you together all night at Phrynion's?"

"Minta and I dined and drank with Phrynion and his hired thugs. Excuse me, Theo, at that time I thought you were one of them. We played and sang for them. I hoped to keep the party going until they drank themselves into a stupor, but I did not succeed." Mama spoke quietly. "Minta, what happened to you?"

"After we sent Phano off to Theo's farm, they took me to the slaves' quarters." Minta shrugged. "No bruises," she added lightly, "and they found me a bed." Something had happened, I could tell. Mama saw it too, but she just nodded.

"This is my fault." Theo sounded wretched. "Whatever harm came to any of you, I was part of it. I offered Phrynion the use of my family farm, thinking you would hardly look for your wife and daughter there, Stephanos. I took Phano there myself, and precious little protection I gave her. I left Nera and Minta for Phrynion. Nera, whatever happened, I am so very sorry."

Mama gathered her dignity like a cloak. "Phrynion stayed for several hours with me," she announced. "We had much to discuss." Father's face turned an ugly, mottled purple. He clenched his fists, but did not speak. If he bit his tongue at that moment, it surely bled.

Mama continued, "I suggest that you accept what we tell you, Husband. Phrynion is a miser, but he is not a fool. Only a fool would have injured our girl under his own roof, where it could easily be proved against him."

The purple left Father's face as quickly as it had come, leaving him white and shivering. "You and I will talk, my dear," he told Mama. The love was there in his voice and his eyes. Mama knew it too. Her hand crept toward him, and his big fist closed around her fingers. Whatever Mama had had to endure from Phrynion, Father loved her not one bit the less.

*Love will keep you warm at night.* The thought flashed through my mind. *But love will not feed you. Love will not keep you or your children safe. What will, then? Respectability, right deeds, a good marriage, surely—or so it seemed to me—and the blessing of the gods. From our birth, we are in their hands.*

There was a long silence. Father broke it at last. "Phrynion has named Aris, son of Nicanor, as his man," he told us. "Do you know him, Theo? What is he like?"

"A good negotiator," said Theo at once. "I can work with him. If you agree, I'll ride ahead and look for him. The sooner we start, the sooner we'll finish."

"Go on, then," said Father. Theo stopped the cart, climbed down and untied his horse. He nodded at Father and put his horse to a gallop, riding on the grassy verge of the road to save us from breathing his dust.

"I like that man," said Mama.

"Theo? A man of action, isn't he, as well as sense. I wish we had met in a different way. He's a member of

35

Council, well respected, I've inquired: Theogenes, son of Demetrios of Alopeke, grandnephew of Nikos, it's an excellent family. Theo could become an archon before the year is up, if the gods are kind." Father was recovering; there was energy in his voice.

"A councilor, maybe an archon: excellent." Mama purred like a cat lapping the richest cream. "Phano likes him, don't you, my girl?" She chuckled. "If I'm not mistaken, our daughter here already dreams of her wedding night. Shall we invite Theo to a little party for her fourteenth birthday? We might be celebrating the end of Phrynion's nonsense that day, who can tell? Don't glare at me, Phano, you are dreaming of him; you know I'm right."

I turned my back on her. She was right, but I would not tell her so. Besides, Theo already had a promised bride.

# five

Theo and Aris agreed on Saurias of Lamptrai as the umpire. I had to be a witness. Theo coached me. "It's not like being in court," he said.

"I couldn't be in court."

"Of course not, you're a woman. This is different. I will ask you about your mother's life with Phrynion, promises he made, whether he kept them or not, things you heard and saw."

"Do I have to tell about my life?" I remembered how cold I was then, hungry, scared. What would Theo think of me if he knew I had slept with the pigs? Would he see a disgusting pig-girl every time he looked at me? Or, even worse, would he pity me? Either way, I didn't want him to know.

"I don't think so," Theo replied. "There are three issues here. Phrynion advanced fifteen minas, which Nera paid to the two men who owned her in Corinth. He says he bought her. She says that money was a gift, and only half the price of her freedom. She raised the rest, ten minas as a gift from the two men when they married, and five from other sources. That's the first thing. Nera ran away from Phrynion—twice, didn't she? The second time, she took furniture, household linens, even the cooking pots, as well as her clothes and jewels, and the three slaves. Phrynion wants the household goods and slaves returned, along with any clothes and jewels that he provided, or the full value in money. That's the second thing."

"This is too much," I snapped. "Two slaves belonged to Mama. We've owned Minta forever. Obole was a gift to her from Phrynion. The gateman belonged to Phrynion, but we did not steal him. Truly, we tied him up and left him behind. It's not Mama's fault if he got loose and followed our tracks.

"Mama deserved everything! Phrynion said he would give her three myrtle wreaths, all gilded; two bronze mirrors, one with a gold Eros for a handle; four pairs of earrings, heavy gold, one with birds, one set with precious stones, one with acorns and oak leaves, and one with lapis and carved ivory."

"He gave her one pair of earrings, gold leaf on alabaster, not real gold at all," Theo chimed in, laughing. "Your mama told you her woes a time or two, I think. Well, you can tell it to Aris and Saurias tomorrow."

He had gone by the time I remembered he had said there were three issues to be settled. What was the third?

❈

I found out soon enough the next day. Mama and Father were to testify that morning; they had not returned when Theo arrived to escort me to the temple. I didn't see much of it. The courtyard was enormous. A huge plane tree would have offered welcome shade in summer.

We met in a small chamber near the entrance. There was a carved chair for Saurias, the umpire, and stools or benches for everybody else. Saurias stood to greet me. I knew him a little; he was a thoughtful, quiet man, his face wrinkled, his beard gray. My first impression of Aris did not change later: more rooster than man, always strutting, always crowing.

Everything they asked me, I answered as best I could, but I did not know much about the fifteen minas. Phrynion treated Minta and me as slaves when we lived with him, but not Mama, even though he locked her door. If money had to be paid, I did not know where it might come from. For sure, our little household had none to spare.

"I have good news for you, Phano," said Saurias when I had finished. "Nera was freed in Corinth before you were born. We have seen her documents, all witnessed and in order. As far as you are concerned, it does not matter whether Phrynion's fifteen minas was a gift to your mother or a loan to help her buy her freedom: you are not the child of a slave."

I stared at him. "Of course I am not the child of a slave."

"That is what I said."

"I am not the child of a freedwoman either," I said sharply. "Mama is my stepmother, my father's second wife. I have known no mother but Nera, but I am the daughter of two citizens of Athens. Phrynion never had any rights over me. We told him often enough."

Theo's mouth was open like the others. I give him credit, though: he was the first to shut it. "This can be proved? Why didn't you tell me?"

"It never occurred to me. If it had come up, I would have told you; so would my father and Mama. My mother died when I was born, fourteen years ago, all but two days. I'm sure it can be proved. Ask Stephanos; she was his wife."

"Thank you," said Theo. "Congratulations on your birthday; I did not realize it was so soon.

"Saurias, could you spare an escort to take Phano home? Let's continue our discussion. I suggest we accept Phano's statement, subject to proof, that she is not Nera's daughter. Phrynion detained an Athenian citizen. He threatened her. He treated her as a slave. She assured her father, in my presence, that she is a virgin. She would not have been, if Phrynion had held her for another day or two."

I left them to it. Mama says Athenians attach too much importance to virginity. If a woman is pregnant when she marries, the marriage is smoother if her husband fathered the child, or if he believes he did. Mama is practical about such things. She does not remember much of Troezen, where she was born, but some women there serve for a time as priestesses in a shrine where any passing traveler may take his comfort with them. A child born to such a priestess is a child of the god. There is no dishonor in it.

Athenians are not the same as the folks in Troezen. Mama has told me if a man should force me against my will, I must tell her at once, but no one else, not then, not ever. She would help me, and then I should forget it, except to put a little blood on my bridal sheets. Mama says any woman who allows her whole life to be ruined by five minutes of some man's nonsense is a fool. She hopes she has not raised a fool.

I hope I am not a fool, but it cannot be as simple as Mama says. I would not want to deceive my husband, when I am married. Surely I could not deceive Theo, if he were to be my husband; it hurt me even to think of it.

❧

Father raged again when I told my story. Mama only laughed. "I shall never fully understand you Athenians," she said. "Who you came from is more important than who you are. If Phano had been born to me instead of an Athenian citizen, she would count for less. I have raised the girl, shouldn't that mean something?

"Let me tell you, Stephanos, your way of thinking will not help Athens to defeat your enemy to the north. Philip of Macedon looks for ability and rewards it. In his army, the best generals are promoted. In his kingdom, accomplishments count for more than family. You call yourself a democracy here in Athens! Hmmm!" Her mouth tightened in disgust.

Father took a deep breath. "This gives Theo an edge. That's good." He must have been right. Theo did not come to see us that evening or the following day, but on the morning of the third day, he arrived. Father and Mama received him. Soon afterward, Mama sent for me.

They were arguing when I arrived. "This is not suitable for a young woman to hear," Theo said.

"Indeed?" Mama snorted. "Phano has not had a protected childhood, as you may have observed; she turns fourteen today. Whatever is decided, she will have to live with it. She deserves to hear."

"Thank you, Mama," I interjected.

Theo stopped objecting. "Stay then, Phano," he said. "Happy birthday! I hoped to find a gift for you, but believe me, there has been no time." He flung out an arm as if pushing something behind him.

"Before I tell you anything more," he continued, "you should all know that Phrynion came to me at night, with an offer. I turned him down. It taught me something about the man I did not know. It made a difference to the result, no doubt of that. I hope you won't blame me for refusing him."

"This is mysterious," Father replied.

"Nothing nasty about that man would surprise me," said Mama. "Was it bribery or blackmail?"

"A bit of both," Theo replied. "You know him well, Nera. He wants me on his side. This was his offer: it would not be enough that I'd stop working to build new ships and repair the long walls; I would have to work to end democracy in Athens. In return, he said he would withdraw his suit and would undertake never to bring suit against Stephanos in future; also, he would drop all claims against you, Nera, now and for all time to come. For me, he promised my bride's dowry would be doubled—and it's generous already."

"He is disgusting," I blurted out.

"He is," Mama agreed. "We knew that. You have made him your enemy as well as ours." She watched Theo quietly.

"You had to turn him down," Father said. "No matter what."

"I don't really want to be related to him by marriage," said Theo. "However, that is not your concern. The proposal I have for you, of course, is not nearly as good as the one Phrynion held out. You won't like everything about it, by any means. We three arbitrators have agreed, however. So now I'll talk as your negotiator.

"Let me review: Phrynion charged that Stephanos stole Nera from him and made a free woman of her, and therefore also robbed him of her daughter, Phano. Further, Stephanos received the goods and the slaves that Nera stole from him when she left.

"This is our judgment: Nera is to be free and her own

43

mistress. Phrynion has no claim on Phano, who in fact is not Nera's child. Everything Nera took from Phrynion's house must be returned, except the clothes and jewelry that were bought for Nera herself, and the maidservant who was also bought for her. The next part is worse: Nera must spend the same number of days each month with Stephanos and Phrynion, unless they both agree to some other arrangement, and the man she is living with must support her while they are together. In the future, Stephanos and Phrynion must be friendly and bear each other no malice."

My mouth fell open. "How could you agree to this?"

"My wife!" Father was shocked.

"Oh, I'm not a citizen wife, am I?" Mama's voice had an edge. "This is your Athenian idea of freedom, to make me spend half my time with a brute and a bully. Well, he's rich. Don't look so downcast, Theo. You were right to refuse his bribe. I assume you'll make sure that he does not beat me or my slaves, and that he feeds us well. If I know Phrynion, he'll want to show me off to his friends while he has the chance to boast. I expect I'll get some parties out of it."

"Mama!" But Mama had kept quiet long enough. Now she was in full flow, the river bursting its banks.

"This does not suit your notions of respectability, does it, Phano? It does not suit my ideas of decency."

"Nor mine," Theo agreed. "That fifteen minas was the sticker. There was nothing to show absolutely it was a gift to you and not a loan. If you had been able to pay him something, ten minas, even five, I could have taken a different path. I would have lent it to you if I could. I am sorry, all of you, but it was the best I could do. Frankly, I doubt the arrangement will last long. It's a way for Phrynion to save face—and to boast, Nera, as you say."

"Look at it another way," said Nera. "It's a brilliant political move for *us*, planting a spy in the enemy camp. Let Phrynion take me to a few dinners with his cronies, and I'll know exactly what they're up to. How amusing! Did you think of that, Theo? I had not thought you were so devious."

"I'm not! It never occurred to me. Nera, you must not do anything so dangerous."

Mama was slightly appeased. " 'Must not'? When you know me better, Theo, you will not use those words to me. He's not a threat to Phano anymore; I'm glad of that."

This new arrangement *was* a threat, though in a different way. Father saw it, just as I did. "My wife lives with another man, dines with him in public! Respectability has gone out the window. Everyone will know. My daughter is almost of age to marry. What family will look at Phano as a bride?"

"Save your sympathy for me," Mama snapped. "Respectability is the excuse Athenian men use to keep women down. You two are no better than the rest of them. I spit on respectability. You are right, Theo, money is our problem—lack of money, I mean. I have been trying to eat respectability, wear respectability. Give me clothes, money, property, jewels, and I can *buy* respectability. Someday I'll show you exactly how it's done.

"Athenian law is interesting, isn't it? One man, Phrynion, sues another man, Stephanos. I, a woman, did not bring this suit. It was not brought against me. Yet I lose my freedom, half my freedom, because of it. What have you learned, Phano?"

"You want me to say it's better to be born a man. A man with money. A citizen. But the gods made me a woman, Mama. I'm not sorry. I don't think you're sorry either."

"For me or you? Either way, you are right."

"I admire both of you more than I can say. I won't speak about respectability, Phano; it's a dangerous word in this household, but you certainly have my respect." Theo stood up to leave. "I take it that you accept this judgment." He looked at Father, but it was Mama who replied.

"We accept."

# SIX

The rest of my birthday passed quietly. Mama gave me her gold earrings with little geese dangling from the hoops.

"My favorites. How did you know?" I jumped up and hugged her.

Mama laughed. "They suit you better than they suit me. You need something to wear with your yellow tunic. Perhaps you and your father will be invited to accompany his family to this year's drama festival. You must be able to make an appearance."

Father gave me an ivory bobbin. "My mother was a weaver," he told me. "This belonged to her. I found it in the loft of this house."

47

"Why give it to me *now*?"

Father shook his head. "It's hard to say. I've kept it by my bed. When I stroke it, I can almost see her at work, with her quick fingers flashing through the long threads, then moving quietly to batten the fabric and make it firm. This bobbin helped me not to worry about what would happen if Phrynion found us. *When* Phrynion found us. Now that he *has* found us, I don't need it anymore. It was always meant to be yours."

"That is her loom in the loft, isn't it?"

"In the other room? Yes, do you want to use it?"

"Of course I do. She left her weaving, a blanket half done. I hoped it might be my grandmother's work. I've wanted to finish it for months. It's dusty, but the threads are good."

"You could have asked me, Daughter."

"Oh, Father, I didn't want to ask, when you were so worried. I thought it would make you sad, thinking about her."

Father blinked back tears. "Finish her work. I'd like you to do that."

For some time after the judgment, Theo did not appear at our home. Two weeks passed, and Mama went to live with Phrynion. Father and I snapped at each other. We both felt lost without her.

"This is my fault," Father said. "I promised to protect her, and I failed."

"What else could you do?"

"I could have asked my family for help. I could still do that."

"Why didn't you?"

"If I have any credit with them at all, I was saving it for you." I raised my eyebrows. He explained. "Where else is your dowry to come from? I haven't done much for the family name, Phano, but I believe our clan will do something for you, if there is a decent marriage to come of it. I doubt they'll help me more than once, though, and they probably would not help Nera. They never wanted me to marry her, you know."

"I haven't helped her either. If I became a courtesan, I could earn money, like Mama when she was young."

"Don't be ridiculous. *My* daughter! I'm a poor man, but I would not allow it, believe me."

"*You* would not allow it."

We faced each other. Father shook his head. "Nera has influenced both of us, Phano. Let's just say your stepmother's business would not suit you. We both know that. It won't suit *her* now either, I'm afraid. I thought I could put up with this wretched arrangement, but I hate to think of her in Phrynion's house. I'm frightened for her. Am I being foolish?"

"You are not being foolish," I told him sadly, "but you are not being practical either."

"Phano, come with me to the family. For Nera. To beg for their help."

I went with him. Cousin Talos and Cousin Anax received us. Talos was small and skinny, with a pale, pointed face. Anax was fat and pink, with rolls of chins and almost no neck. They looked me over, as if I were a horse they thought of buying.

"You should bring your daughter to family events," said Anax. "Our wives and daughters will be pleased to meet you, Phano." They refused to discuss business in my presence. Their wives and daughters might want to meet me, but not that day. I sat with the housekeeper and fretted. If Father had been five minutes longer, I would have had a borrowed spindle in my hand.

Father was polite and distant while we said farewell, but the gate had barely closed behind us before he told me we'd made our trip for nothing. "My wife is a disgrace to the family. I'm a disgrace to the family. I can't repay the money they have lent already, let alone more. If I go bankrupt, it will be a worse disgrace to the family, but they still won't help. I made a fool of myself, and all for nothing. Worse than nothing: I've created ill will for you. Their wives and daughters won't be inviting *you* to join them at family events."

"I wouldn't go without Mama," I said at once.

"That's my girl. Poor but proud. I knew it was useless. I *knew* it, and I still went down on my knees to them. I'm an idiot." He threw back his shoulders. "Don't tell Nera." He sighed. "She'll only ask if she's married a fool."

Mama came home a day or two later. I had expected her to be pale and sad, but she was full of life, as if she had been on a thrilling journey. "Stephanos, we have work to do," she announced. "We'll have an oligarchy again in

Athens if Phrynion has his way. If the rich men control our government, Athens is lost."

"Athens is lost already." Father was gloomy, though relieved that Mama was safe.

"Last time we had an oligarchy, it was Sparta's fault," I said. I knew plenty about oligarchies, thanks to Mama's training. We'd had two of them in Athens, committees of rich men governing us, instead of democracy, where our rulers were chosen by lot.

The Oligarchy of Thirty had made our family poor, so naturally I remembered what I was told about it. Sparta defeated Athens. The conquerors put thirty rich men in power, Athenian men, but puppets of Sparta. Many people plotted against them, Father's grandfather for one. When the government bullies seized their property, the revolt began. The Oligarchy actually sent to Sparta for help. Athenians called on the mortal enemies of Athens for help against other Athenians!

The gods themselves must have been offended. They sent a snowstorm to keep the Spartan soldiers away. The citizens won, and we had democracy again. Unluckily, Stephanos's grandfather caught a bad cold waiting for the Spartans in the snowstorm. The doctors bled him, but the cold went into his chest and he died. If he had lived, Stephanos would have inherited more than the little house. A person might say that Mama had to live part-time with Phrynion because of an oligarchy more than fifty years before. We did not like oligarchies in our family.

"I've learned a thing or two," Mama went on.

"Phrynion and his buddies seem to be afraid of Theo. Certainly he's the man they are watching. The pool of citizens is small this year. Theo could become an archon, just as you said."

"Our Theo, one of the nine? It was an idle thought, nothing as real as you suggest. Wonders will never cease." Father brightened. "He would do well, wouldn't he? Not that it's anything to do with me. Does he know enough law to pass his test?"

"If he does not, we both know who could coach him."

Father laughed. Athenian law has been his hobby since childhood. No case stumped him, however obscure. It was his modest claim to fame, that lawyers came from time to time to consult privately with him. He did not speak about their discussions with me or anyone else except Mama, though I knew he talked to her. He had to be discreet, or the lawyers would have stopped coming to him for advice.

Father offered his help, and soon Theo began to visit our little house almost every day. He usually came in the morning. Father coached him. Mama joined them, until she had to go back to live with Phrynion again. When Mama was at home, the coaching sessions included me.

Politics and the laws of Athens have never been my favorite studies. I saw little use in such subjects for my future as a wife. "Teach me to make your Egyptian honey cakes,"

I used to tell Mama, "or a love potion, or a purge if the slaves are ill. Something practical."

Because of Theo, I discovered new aspects of the study of law and politics, some of them more interesting than honey cakes or laxatives. When Mama went to live with Phrynion again, Father and Theo worked by themselves. Sometimes they came to see me before Theo left. "My wedding is off," Theo announced one day. "Did I speak about it before?"

"Twice," I reminded him. "Once at your farm, and again when you turned down Phrynion's offer. He was going to double her dowry, which was already generous." I repeated his words exactly, even the way he spoke. "She was a relative of Phrynion's, wasn't she?" I pretended to be casual.

"She was. I only met her twice, but she is as dull as any woman I've ever tried to talk to. I thought perhaps she was merely shy, or modest, so I asked my cousin, who knows her. Demi says Chloe seldom puts two words together, and they're not worth hearing when she does."

"That's no reason to reject a promised bride," I said.

"True enough. Perhaps a different match would suit me better. If it was a good alliance, though, my family would want me to complete it." He paused. "Nikos, son of Diodoros, is head of my clan. I'd like you to meet him sometime. He is a grand old man, my great-uncle. He never liked Phrynion much. His son Bardian arranged the match with Chloe. When I told Uncle about Phrynion's bribe, he withdrew his approval. Bardian is furious, but that makes no difference. As long as Uncle keeps his voice and his wits, he speaks for the family. I'm thankful, as I have changed my mind as well."

"Husband and wife usually learn to love each other after they are married." I spoke stiffly.

"That did not happen between me and your mother." Father sighed. "Phano, you were the only good result of that marriage."

"They arrange things differently in Sparta," said Theo. "Men and women are much the same age when they marry. If they lived together, they might be good companions. Why should a man have to wait until he is thirty, the way we do in Athens?"

I think thirty is a good age for a husband, and fifteen a good age for a bride. Spartans don't care about anything except fighting, as far as I know. "Don't husband and wife live together in Sparta?" I asked. "Surely they must, some of the time."

Theo nodded. "The young husband comes home for a few hours, until his wife is pregnant, but he sleeps in the barracks with his mates. Would you like such a marriage, Phano?"

I would not, and had no hesitation in saying so. Father, looking very pleased with himself, escorted Theo to the door.

Now that we weren't so worried about Mama, the two weeks passed quickly, and she came home again, as bright and lively as I had ever seen her. "I like this spy business," she announced. "It's a new career, and it suits me well. When I've squeezed every bit of information out of Phrynion, perhaps I'll journey to Macedon. I've a fancy to join Philip's household. I should be welcome there, a cultured woman like me, don't you think?"

Father glared at her. "Before you rush off to Macedon, *Wife*"—he leaned on the short word—"kindly tell us what you have gleaned from Phrynion."

"Not much, actually," Mama had to admit. "He has his hand in the treasury where he shouldn't, but I have no proof of that. If you had the connections to arrange an audit, it would probably show up. He has sent out messengers and received messengers, as he did before. A northern accent again. Talk, talk, talk at the dinners, all about new alliances, looking forward, not looking back, forging the future of Athens, a lot of hot air.

"It's easy enough to see he was talking about Philip, and Macedon, and giving away our independence, but the words were never spoken, and I cannot claim they were. Hot air." Mama grinned. "I do enjoy going to parties again," she added. "I've missed the excitement. Minta will have to massage away some of this fat." She pushed back her sleeve and pinched the flesh of her upper arm.

"I've been gobbling up meat, roast suckling pig, haunches of beef and venison, legs of lamb; and birds, little quail by the dozen, chickens, ducks; figs and pomegranates as well as apples and pears; soft cheeses and hard cheeses made from the milk of goats, or sheep, or cows;

clams and flounders from the sea, as well as other fish. When I think of all the lentil stew I've eaten in this house, Stephanos, I do enjoy the change."

"Would you rather eat meat with Phrynion or lentil stew with me?"

"A difficult choice. Our arbitrators did well to present me with both." Mama was teasing, and Father's glare made her tease him more. "How lucky for me, that judgment! I enjoy meat, as you know full well, and I enjoy a change from time to time. Perhaps we'll eat meat here someday. Meanwhile, I'm tired of rich food and parties, and happy to be home." Her voice turned tender. "Happy to be with the man I love, my darling, and with my girl, as close to a daughter as I'll ever have. So tell me, what has been happening here? Anything important?"

I badly wanted to let Mama change the subject, but I had to change it back again; I couldn't let it rest. "I don't understand what's going on with Phrynion," I started.

"He's got what he wants, and he's rubbing my nose in it, that's obvious," Father snarled.

"Is that all? I don't know. Phrynion is not like he was before. Why? It makes me nervous."

"It's not that much of a change," Mama replied. "He never whipped *me*, if you remember. Never slapped me around either, like you and Minta. Some men feed on a woman's fear; Phrynion is one of them. You are afraid of him; I'm not. Careful, yes, I have not lost my wits, but there's no terror for him to smell on me."

"And the parties? All that meat? Phrynion hated to

spend an obol. Now he is throwing parties himself, as well as taking you to dine with his friends. That's a new pair of earrings you're wearing. From him? Real gold, I'm sure, you would not wear fakes."

Mama bent her neck to show off the heavy gold hoops. "He wants to make your father miserable, no doubt," she said. "So don't let Phrynion see it, or hear of it, if he succeeds. He likes to show me off. He'd like it better if I was meek and chastened, but he'd wonder what I was up to if I began to act like that. Anyway, it would not be so much fun."

"You *like* this, Nera."

"It's the best fun I've had in years," Mama agreed. "You are jealous, Stephanos." She laughed.

"Mama, that's cruel!" But I had to chuckle too.

Minta came in. Theo was at the door, wondering if Mama was home, and if all was well. Theo was nervous, like me. He moved right into our conversation. "Phrynion is not spending his own money, that's my belief," he said. "How much is it worth to Philip, to keep Athens weak? Phrynion would be his ideal stooge. I'm not usually a betting man, but I'd wager gold that Philip of Macedon is bribing him. Watch Phrynion, Nera. See if he pays in philippeioi."

"Nothing so obvious," Mama replied. "Don't think I've not watched. He uses some coins of Macedon, but no more than an honest citizen might. I'll make an excuse to see his treasury next time."

Theo could not stay; he was already late for a meeting.

He turned at the door. "Be careful, Nera, he's a dangerous man."

"Certainly," Mama airily agreed, sending the word after Theo's vanishing back. She turned to us. "But I've tamed the tiger, you'll see."

I wished I could be as sure of that as Mama was.

# seven

"Theo has made himself at home here, that's easy to see." Mama's eyes sparkled with mischief. "Take care, Phano. If I were his bride-to-be, I'd scratch out your eyes."

"You put things so delicately." Father chuckled. I felt the flush burning my cheeks. "Well, my dear, Theo's bride-to-be won't be attacking Phano, you'll be pleased to hear. That marriage is off."

"Ahhhh." Mama stretched the syllable into a sentence.

"Yes," Father continued. "Your instincts for romance have never failed, Nera. Theo goes on about wedding customs in Sparta, but he's talking to Phano. Our daughter dreams of him as well."

"Indeed. You may make a respectable marriage in spite of your mama. For your sake, Phano, I wish it may be so. How can your father and I help? I must think about this."

"Perhaps he likes me, Mama. I hope he does. But Theo is a family man. His family would have to agree to any marriage. I hardly think they'd welcome *me* as his bride."

Mama shrugged. "You are of an age to marry. We must do what we can. Husband, we must send this girl to be a Little Bear of Artemis. Isn't that what Athenians do?"

"Yes, to the sanctuary at Brauron, on the coast. My mother was a Little Bear. She loved it. We are too much cut off from proper ways of doing things, Nera; I'm glad you reminded me of this."

"What do you mean, a Little Bear of Artemis? Brauron is a huge distance, more than a day's journey. Mama, Father, don't send me away."

"No matter, if you want to be a proper wife, this is a proper thing to do. I don't know much about it, but it cannot be dark and horrible or I would have heard."

When Mama makes up her mind, things happen. She began by sending Minta to the market. Slaves don't have power, but if they are allowed to go out, there isn't much they can't discover. Minta has her cronies. She came home with a bag of onions, an enormous cabbage and all the information we needed.

"You must arrange things with the priestesses here," Minta told us. "Phano is citizen born, it won't be difficult.

You must make a gift to the shrine, though, money or jewelry, something valuable, even if our young mistress only goes for two weeks. That's the shortest time."

"Two weeks is enough," Mama decided. "We'll dedicate my topaz ring. The jewel doesn't really suit me, and the priestesses will be pleased."

Father went to the temple the following day. Nine new Little Bears were to leave for Brauron in three days. I would be the tenth.

Summer heat had already invaded Athens. In spite of my nervousness, I was happy to leave the hot, sticky city for the cool woodland track.

Ten new Little Bears jolted along together, five of us to a cart. In each cart a man held the reins, but he never turned to look at us. A priestess of Artemis sat beside each driver. They might have been twins: tall, thin women, with skin leathery and dark from the sun.

The others chattered away. I kept quiet, not knowing what was safe to say. I asked a question once or twice, hoping not to be thought unfriendly, but that prompted questions in return, so I gave it up. We spent two days traveling, and the time dragged, less so on the second day when the road took us along the shore. Far out, the sun made diamond sparkles in the great ocean; nearby, waves crashed on the dark rocks.

There must have been twenty girls already at Brauron when we arrived. I'd never lived with a crowd like that before. We were much of an age, some younger than I and a few older, but only by a few months. Many of them knew the names and family of the men they were to marry, and some knew the wedding date. Others were like me. We all served Artemis. When Artemis visits the earth, she may take the form of a bear. Bears are sacred to her. That's why we were called Little Bears.

One other girl was quiet, like me, though very different in looks. I was on the tall side of medium height, but she was huge, outsized and muscular, with arms like hams, her fair skin reddened by the sun. She was more of a bear than anyone else, though one could hardly call her little. She had already spent two weeks at the sanctuary; she was to remain for two weeks more. Her name was Boulete; everybody called her Bouly. Her name meant "wanted."

All of us Little Bears slept on mattresses of straw in two big rooms. Bouly's mattress lay beside mine. I had mostly finished my monthly cycle when I arrived; so had she, as it turned out. She showed me where to find the latrines, then took me to the stream to wash out my soiled cloths and underclothes. After two days of travel, I had nothing clean. Bouly found two or three extra pieces of cloth from her own supply, in case mine did not dry soon enough. I had never shared something so intimate with anyone except Mama.

Bouly and I might have become friends even if Theo had not entered into it, but he did. As Bouly and I began to speak about our families, I discovered that Theo was her cousin. "So you are the girl he talked about." Bouly grinned.

"What did he tell you? The truth, mind you—don't make it prettier on my account."

"Nothing much, truly. You are the daughter of a friend who knows the laws and codes of Athens from the time of Solon to the present day. He said more about your father than about you. Mind you, he was talking to my father, not to me. His eyes looked soft, like a cow's eyes, when he said his friend had a daughter who knew a lot about politics and history, more than many men. My father did not know whether to believe it or not. 'If that's true,' he said, 'she has been badly brought up.'

"'Come now, Uncle,' Theo objected, 'how can you say that?' Then he changed the subject before my father could say any more. They were heading for a big argument. Father is old-fashioned. But Phano, is it true?"

"That I've been badly brought up?"

"Of course not. About politics. Mama says it's deadly dull; I know I start to yawn when Theo and my father get going. We don't have to pay to build ships for Athens. Father says that's lucky, as it will take a big dowry to marry me off. Theo says Father and his brothers should build a trireme and equip her for battle, even if they don't have to."

"I thought every family had to, if they were rich enough." I stared at her.

"Father and his brothers did not divide the property when my grandfather died. They own it together. That's why they get an exemption from the shipbuilding levy. Theo says it's not right; his family divided their property, and they get taxed. That's why he's poor, he says."

"You know a lot about politics, Bouly," I said, "as much as me, I think."

"Only about my own family, and that's dull enough, except for my dowry. I am so big, do you think any man will marry me?"

"Does it matter?" I sounded just like Mama.

"Getting married? Phano, you're teasing me. Don't you want to be married and have babies? I do."

"So do I, Bouly. I hope the gods grant us both our wish."

My hands itched for a basket of wool and a spindle, but I could see nothing of that kind. Artemis is the goddess of maidens, not of wives, of running and the hunt, not of home and hearth. Soon, however, I settled in. All Little Bears competed in running, by ourselves and in teams; also in archery, in throwing a ball and catching it, even in swimming. Bouly and I tried to be on the same team when we could.

I did well enough to be accepted, nothing more. Bouly was strong as well as big: no one else could bend a man's bow; her arrows flew twice as far as mine and hit the target while mine went wide. Bouly killed a hare one day, and skinned and cooked it as well. Bouly pulled another girl out of the ocean when she would have drowned.

"I have an enemy," I told her. "Would you help me against him if I needed you?"

"I never had an enemy." Bouly sounded disappointed. "Your life is so interesting, Phano. It would be an adventure, helping you."

"It might be dangerous." I felt guilty. She was positively eager.

"That wouldn't stop me! Who is he? Maybe I know him."

If I told her Phrynion's name, I'd have to tell her a lot more. What would she think of me if she knew I had lived like a slave in Phrynion's house? "It's better if you don't know his name, unless I need your help. Thank you, Bouly, all the same. I feel better protected, knowing you."

Near the end of my stay spindles and wool appeared, and there was a spinning bee. Apparently Artemis did not despise that skill, although she has never been known to practice it. Lacking my thigh shield, I stood to my work, and the wool slipped through my fingers, twisting into a fine even yarn. Soon the air rang with praise: "How much you've done already, Phano!" "So even!" "So quick!" "It's beautiful."

The priestesses themselves were delighted. "We have nothing to teach you," one of them laughed. "You might teach some of us! Skill such as yours is the result of natural ability and of long practice both. Good teaching helps someone like you to avoid bad habits, but you have no bad habits in your spinning. This is a great skill, Phano; it will bring renown. Your husband, when you marry, will boast of you."

I blushed. "It is Athene's gift." However, for the rest of my short stay, I was the most popular Little Bear at the sanctuary. All the girls wanted to watch me and to have me watch them, to help them improve. It was a heady joy, to be so admired—and respected. If a flower has feelings, this is how it must feel when the sun warms the bud and the blossom unfolds.

I tried not to slight Bouly, but it was difficult. When I left, we promised to visit each other later. "I'll steer Theo in the right direction." Bouly laughed. "Then we can be cousins as well as friends."

"I have never had a friend." *Only Minta, I thought, a slave woman; she is not exactly a friend.* It seemed disloyal to Minta, who had looked after me all my life; but if I had to choose, I knew I would choose Bouly, whom I'd known less than two weeks.

The journey back to Athens took the same time as before, but it felt as if only minutes had gone by when we approached the city. Waves of heat shimmered up from the baked mud of the track, and then from the stones of the city streets. I hugged everyone when I jumped down at our own door.

Father and I were alone together that evening. Mama had been with Phrynion for half a week, no more, but he was very lonely. We talked about Brauron and Little Bears. I told him about my new friend Bouly. He asked a question or two about her family, but he hardly listened to my replies. His face was tired. Soon his head drooped on the cushions.

Banging and shouting at the gate roused us both. We ran downstairs. Phrynion's bully boy entered. A limp figure, wrapped in a cloak, was draped over his shoulder. I knew it was Mama even before I saw the red-gold curls. He threw her down on the flagstones like a sack of meal. "Master says he's done with her, she's not to come back," he sneered. "She drank more wine than was good for her and fell down the stairs. A pity."

"Mama!" I knelt beside her and drew the cloak aside. She was wearing a red tunic, one I did not recognize. Then I looked again. I knew this garment, but it had been white, embroidered by Minta with gold and silver leaves. Now it was soaked with blood.

Mama's right hand held a piece of cloth against her mouth. Her hand was cold, and I put both my hands around it to warm it. Fresh blood welled from her split lips. She opened her mouth. There was a black gap where her front teeth had been. Father made some noise, like an animal in pain. Mama's dark eyes opened wearily. She tried to speak. Her tongue was hugely swollen. When she did manage to speak, the words were thick and slurred. "No more spying," I think she said. Then her head fell back.

"Mama!" I screamed. I was certain she was dead. Her eyes fluttered open, then closed again.

We had no money to pay the doctor. Father sent Minta to pawn Mama's new earrings before he would come. Mama's left leg was broken, and he set it and tied boards on both sides to hold it in place. He wanted to bleed her too, but Minta begged Father not to let him. "Phrynion has bled her, more than enough," she insisted.

Mama's nose was broken, and her mouth was ruined. Dear Mama, she would never be beautiful again. Father and I did not care at all. She was alive. She would recover. It would have been mean of Father, but I think he might have been a little bit glad. No man would give him reason for jealousy now.

We never did get the story clearly. Just bits and pieces over the next days and weeks. Mama had been hot on the trail of proof that Phrynion was in league with Philip of Macedon, and Phrynion had caught her. "Stupid woman," he taunted. "I had not thought you were so stupid. I knew from the start what you were doing, spying on me. I set a trap, and you fell right into it." He made it sound as if he had pretended to be a traitor to Athens to catch her.

Phrynion had not touched Mama himself. The beating had not even happened at his house, but in a little room at a brothel; Father looked sick when Mama said the name of it. "Where will you go to make your complaint?" I asked. "Phrynion deserves a worse beating than poor Mama. What will happen to him?"

"Nothing will happen. I won't make a fool of myself by lodging a complaint." Father shook his head. "Would anyone arrest a rich and powerful man because a woman of no reputation was beaten in an ill-reputed place? His bully boys will be as well protected as he is, you can count on it. There's nothing to be done."

"You sound as if Phrynion had beaten you as well as Mama," I told him. I felt angry and scared.

"He has beaten me," Father replied. "He has beaten all of us. What's worse, I suspect he is not finished yet."

"Mama would tell you to be brave, our turn will come."

"Maybe. We'll soon find out if she still talks like that."

# eight

We nursed Mama while her body slowly healed. Minta searched for herbs, some for poultices, others for teas to drink. She brought back peppermint from the marshes, chamomile and pungent oregano. She taught me the safe use of poppy to induce a soothing sleep.

Theo came from time to time, less often as the days went by. I had little time or energy for him. If he felt I was indifferent, he had cause. The business and political life of Athens absorbed him, the way Mama's needs absorbed me. I had no business letting myself dream of marriage to Theo, and the dream faded as the days went by. It had always been a foolish fantasy.

When the lots were cast that year, Theo became a

member of the Areopagos. That in itself would not have been enough to rule out marriage to an unimportant girl like me. Most citizen men could expect to serve. That position did not overawe me. But the time came for the Council of Five Hundred to be chosen; then lots were drawn to select the nine Archons of Athens. Suddenly, Theo was King Archon, the Basileus, one of the nine.

Swearing an oath by the Archons of Athens is as potent as swearing by the gods. All nine of them are equal in power and in their heavy duties to the city, although three of them have special duties and special names. The Polemarch is responsible for foreigners in Athens; that means all the people who are not citizens. When Phrynion wanted to be sure Mama did not run away, he charged her before the Polemarch. I am a citizen. If Phrynion had a complaint against me, he would have to charge me before the Basileus. For the coming year that would be Theo, unless he failed the tests for taking such high office.

I had no doubt that he would pass. He was a citizen, the child of citizen parents for three generations on both sides. He had been accepted by his own father as a baby, and had been accepted by his extended family and his clan, with all the proper ceremonies, at all the proper times. He had never failed in his duties to the state, to the gods or to his parents. Stephanos had coached him in the niceties of law.

"Theo lacks only one thing," Father told me, "a wife. He will have to marry very soon."

"We must wish him happiness," I said.

"We must wish him *you*," Mama replied. She pushed herself up from the pile of pillows on the couch and thumped her walking stick on the floor.

"Stephanos, now is the time to see your cousins again. You need a loan. Theo has appointments to make: his Magistrates' Board, two assessors. You want to be a member of his board; you want to be one of his assessors. Sometimes it takes money to make money, Stephanos, your cousins are well aware of that! They have not lent you money in the past, but with these appointments you will be able to repay them and do well for all of us. The daughter of a respected assessor can certainly become the Basilinna."

I was confused. "You didn't want Father to be a tax collector. Isn't an assessor the same?"

"Certainly not. Everybody hates tax collectors. That was a silly idea, even if the money for it had not been stolen."

"You didn't put it that way at the time," said Father stiffly.

"Of course not, my darling. You and that idiot had made your plan. You would hardly have listened to me. Then it blew up in our faces, and you were gone. Well, past is past, I always say. We work together these days, don't we?"

"What is different about this plan?" I asked. Mama liked plans she made better than plans made by other people, perhaps because her plans almost always succeeded. She gave another reason for liking this one.

"Think for a minute, Phano. It's not at all the same. This time, your father has a trusted friend in the highest office: Theo."

"I hate to go begging to my relatives." I knew why Father sounded so bitter, but Mama, of course, did not. She stared at him.

"It's an excellent plan," she said. "You won't have to beg. Your cousins will see at once that it's good for them as well as us."

"Nothing to be lost but pride, I suppose," said Father. He shrugged. "We'd know where the money is coming from," he added. "If it comes."

"It may be fine for you two." I faced Mama. "And for me as the daughter in this house. But for me to marry the King Archon? Mama, you cannot be serious about that."

"I am completely serious."

"So am I." Father jumped up and patted my shoulder on his way to Mama's side. He swung her to her feet, whirled her round and nestled her into the cushions again without pausing for a breath. "If this works out, Nera, it will solve all our problems. Even better, it will be good for Athens. I know I can serve her well. This will have to move fast. I'd best see my cousins at once."

To my amazement (and his own as well), Father came home with his loan. Now he set himself to raise money for Theo's expenses. Within a week, Theogenes, son of Demetrios of Alopeke, was confirmed as Basileus; and Stephanos, son of Crito, my father, had become his assessor and a member of his board.

We celebrated quietly, Father, Mama and I. That

night I poured an especially generous libation to Hera. "I will serve you always, Goddess," I told her. "Grant me to serve you as Theo's wife."

Did Hera send my dream that night? Athens was the place of it, but Athens a hundred years ago or more. Theo and I were dining with great Pericles himself, and with Aspasia, the woman whom he idolized; no one was present except us four.

The men reclined on couches. Aspasia, robed all in gold and wearing a long necklace of carved ivory beads, sat beside her lover, dropping purple grapes into his open mouth, one by one. I dropped a grape into Theo's mouth, and he pulled me down and kissed me, so that I tasted the grape from his mouth. The taste, and the kiss, went on and on.

Athene's glorious temple, the Parthenon, was nothing more than a grand foundation. As I watched, vast pillars raised themselves, and walls rose too. Stone piled on stone, with neither hands nor ropes to lift them. At the far end, I watched the sculptor, none other than Phidias himself, carve the ivory face of the statue and cast her golden body. Beyond the columns of the Parthenon, I saw her: Athene the Virgin Goddess, twice as tall as a house.

In the way of dreams, the temple rose and the statue shone with gold and ivory, and Aspasia fed grapes to Pericles and I kissed Theo, all at the same time. I was all of it, golden Aspasia, golden Pericles, golden temple, golden goddess, myself and Theo as well—everything was me, and I was everything. I was the glory of Athens.

Time passed in my dream, a year or two, no more. Theo and I still feasted with Aspasia and Pericles, but around us everything had changed. A small gray-green monkey sat beside Aspasia. She stroked it lovingly, but it was a bad-tempered beast; it bit her arm, so that blood flowed. Her beautiful eyes turned red and rheumy. She coughed up blood. Her skin became red and rough, full of ulcers that grew and burst. Her body was her own, but mine as well; I felt her agony.

Pericles still ruled in Athens, but the people who had loved him once now hated him. They pelted him with rotten fruit if he walked abroad, even though his two sons had both died of the plague. Those were his sons from his marriage to his citizen wife. Aspasia was a courtesan; she could never be a proper wife.

People said that Aspasia was the real power in Athens, not Pericles. He loved her. He did what she wanted. They had made Athens great together. Perhaps they had been too proud. The gods are angry when people are too proud.

A boy in a white tunic came into the room. He ran to Aspasia. She pushed him away. I knew she longed to hug him. The pain of her longing was as dreadful as the burning pain of her disease. "Keep our son away from me," she commanded hoarsely. "Keep him away from everybody who is ill, or dying, or dead. Keep him safe."

Pericles held the boy. How he loved Aspasia! The boy did not get the plague, but of course he could not be a citizen, a courtesan's son! Pericles changed the laws. For a year, anybody whose father was a citizen would be a citizen as well. Pericles tried to say it was to help Athens, but he really did it because of Aspasia and their son.

"Athens needs more citizens," he said. "So many have died. We have changed our laws before, when Athenian men were killed in battle, or when foreign-born men fought bravely for us. This plague is worse than war."

Theo had disappeared from my dream; then I disappeared from it myself. The glory of Athens was gone forever. I woke up shivering, determined not to fall asleep again. If this was a true dream, what did it signify? Aspasia and Pericles had sought the glory of Athens, but their regime had ended with plague and destruction. Theo and I wanted to save Athens from betrayal and conquest. Would our dream end like theirs?

# nine

My eyes still sticky with sleep, I picked my way across the rough floor of my little loft room to unbar the shutters. Sunrise reddened the whole sky, and the sun came up in a ball of fire. My dream filled me with dread. A year earlier, I would have run to Minta and poured it out to her. She would have comforted me, explained my fears away.

I would have believed her then. Now I knew more, and trusted less. Minta would say anything to make me carefree and happy, like a child. She still wanted to kiss my cuts and bruises and make them better.

I was not a child any longer. My dream was not a cobweb to be brushed away.

That day was Bouly's fourteenth birthday. Only a few

months had passed since mine, but I felt much older than my friend. Father and I were invited to the party, and Mama as well. This was the first time that Father and Mama had been invited to be part of an important event at a respectable family's home. It was also the first time Mama had gone out into company since Phrynion had beaten her. I was certain that Bouly had pestered her father to invite us, but I did not think he would have done so two weeks earlier. Now Father was an important man; it made a difference. I was proud of Mama for deciding to go.

"Did you think I'd let Phrynion stop me?" She stamped her foot furiously, then winced. Mama always used to stamp her left foot when she was angry; too often, she forgot that leg had been broken and did it the same way still. She continued quietly, "They are Theo's relatives. We must all go. Wear something of mine if you like, Phano." Mama had never made such an offer before. She must really want me to impress Theo's relatives!

"Thank you, Mama." I was touched, but I wanted to wear a garment I had made myself. "It would be dreadful if I spilled wine on your linen chiton," I told her, "or tore the hem. Besides, your clothes are too short for me." This was true. They were also too thick about the waist, though I could have chosen one and belted it tight.

I owned only one chiton worthy of the occasion, yellow, like sunflowers. I had gathered seeds myself and dyed the yarn for it, and woven the cloth with stripes of dark red and black to make a border. Minta helped me to gather it along the arms; Mama was hopeless at that work, like much else domestic, but she let me choose the sleeve fastenings out of her own jewelry box, *five* on each side! I found a set of small bronze brooches made in the shape of a goose. Minta spent an hour arranging my hair in the same elaborate style as Mama's, pulled away from my face, gathered high at the back of my head, with glossy ringlets cascading around my neck. Mama's birthday earrings were perfect, as she had known they would be.

A beautiful, elegant woman stared back at me from Mama's bronze mirror. She had my dark brown eyes, but she did not feel like me.

Father hired a small cart with cushions so Mama and I would not drag our clothes in the muck. From the street, Bouly's home looked unpleasantly like Phrynion's house: big and intimidating, with a two-story expanse of wooden walls. I wish that rich people would put windows on the outer-facing walls of their homes, but most of them don't. Mama thought they must be scared of thieves, but Father told her they wanted protection from the mob, if there was rioting in the streets. These days there's not much worry, but the houses have not changed.

As soon as we passed through the gatehouse, however, Bouly's home felt completely different from Phrynion's. Upstairs and down, the rooms around me opened onto gracious balconies. They were full of windows with wide-open shutters.

I spared the building only a quick glance, however, before looking around the courtyard. Sunlight sparkled on a fountain of white marble, with water cascading into a pool. Several small children, naked, splashed each other, screaming in delight. Indeed, most people in the crowd seemed to be shouting happily at one another.

I thought at first the noise would deafen me. Our family is quiet. I have always been the only child. Then Bouly saw me and rushed over. Two younger girls ran after her. "Bouly!" It was a shout of exasperation, from a plump little woman, a smaller, older, neater version of Bouly herself.

"Yes, Mother." Bouly obeyed the unspoken command and slowed to a decorous walk as she approached. She introduced the girls, who turned out to be Theo's young sisters; they giggled at me. I introduced Father and Mama. We whirled into the party, Mama toward Bouly's mother and the other matrons, and Father toward the men sitting on wooden benches or on raised seats of stone. Theo's sisters, still giggling, ran off to play ball with some other girls.

"Come with me," whispered Bouly. Arm in arm, we walked sedately across the expanse of courtyard toward the stairway against the far wall. "Did you hear about Chloe? You know, Phrynion's niece. Theo was supposed to marry her, but he broke it off. Chloe married another friend of Phrynion's," Bouly told me, "but she was pregnant when he married her, only he didn't know, and then he found out and sent her home. That's a low-down trick on your husband, isn't it. Theo says he's lucky he broke it off." Bouly made a face. "Some women have no shame," she added.

What could I say? I felt years and years older than Bouly just then. "A woman cannot always choose," I began. Bouly looked at me oddly. "No, *I* am certainly not pregnant," I said, understanding suddenly why she had looked at me like that. "You are right, Bouly, it is shameful to deceive your husband. I would not do that, any more than you."

Before we could say more, Minta caught up to us, asking us to wait for Mama. Mama progressed across the courtyard like a ship under sail. She wore a full tunic of pure white linen, its soft folds emphasized by the rich purple cloak that wound around her body and fell over her shoulder to billow in the gentle wind. Her golden earrings with the little birdcages and songbirds sparkled and danced as the sunlight caught them; her henna-reddened ringlets blazed. Mama walked slowly. Her left leg had healed a little shorter than before, so she limped, but anyone who did not know would hardly notice it. Her nose was shorter now, and her lips were bigger. I was used to her new face; it did not shock me anymore. When she laughed, there was a black space where her teeth had been, but she didn't laugh as much these days, and she hid her mouth with her hand. Mama had not really changed, though, and I thanked the gods for it.

That morning, Mama had worked for more than an hour with her Egyptian makeup box, applying various colors to her face. The result was interesting, distinguished even. Father had said some people she knew might not recognize her. "A good time to turn respectable, if that's true," Mama had replied.

Mama had always enjoyed attention. Now she walked

as if she did not notice that everybody was watching her, but anyone could tell that was a big act. Mama looked much too interesting to be respectable. I didn't care. Nor, apparently, did Bouly. Mama beckoned us to go with her. "Theo wants to introduce you to the head of his family," she told me.

"Uncle Nikos," said Bouly. "He's old and brown, like a tortoise. You'll like him, Phano."

Would he like me? I wondered.

Uncle Nikos was Theo's great-uncle. He *did* look like an ancient tortoise, peering at me with his head jutting out from his wrinkled neck. His voice was whispery with age. "Phano." His lips pulled back from his gums in a kind of smile. "Theo has told me about you."

"Sir." I did not know what to call him. I dropped my head modestly.

A cackle of laughter bubbled out of the old man's mouth. "Don't be afraid of me, girl," he said, more strongly. "Theo says you are brave, and that you know about politics. Let me test you! Answer me these two questions, if you please. First, what is the greatest danger to Athens at present? Second, what must Athens do to be saved?"

"Come, now, Uncle," Theo put in, laughing and shaking his head, "that's a poor way to get acquainted with a young woman!" Other men's voices joined in, some telling Uncle Nikos those were not questions for any woman to answer, let alone one so young; others telling me to pay no attention, Uncle Nikos was so old he could say what he pleased, but one need not answer him.

Another voice was raised louder than the rest. "Father, you mock the dignity of our family. You tread on our good name." The speaker was a fat, self-important, red-faced man with little pig eyes sunk in his fleshy cheeks. His chins trembled as he talked. He spoke to his father, but he looked straight at me? "You're a bigger fool than he is if you answer him," he said.

I turned to Uncle Nikos. "Sometimes old eyes and young eyes see most clearly," he said quietly.

"I mean no disrespect to anyone in this company," I began slowly. "Yet I wish to answer your questions, Uncle." I waited for the words to form.

"Some people say the greatest danger to Athens comes from the north, from Philip of Macedon. I believe that treachery from within, from our own people, is a greater danger. If the people of Athens stand together, the city will never be conquered. That is the answer to your second question, sir: the people of Athens must stand together. I believe that with all my heart; yet I do not know how it may come to pass, when those who govern us are so bitterly divided."

"Thank you, Phano. She's your daughter, Stephanos? She does you credit. Those are words to ponder, gentlemen. Out of the mouths of children..." His voice trailed off. "Go now, I am tired. Theo, take her away. Bardian, send my man. I am going home."

With Bouly on one side of me and Theo on the other, I walked away very slowly. Bouly's hand on my arm trembled. "I could not have said anything, even if I had known anything to say," she said in a small voice. "Bardian was furious. You knew he would be, didn't you?"

"Bardian is a bully," I replied. "What's worse, he bullies his own father. That is hateful to gods and men. It's hateful to women too," I snapped. Theo had not said anything. I looked up at him. "Maybe I should have kept quiet?" I asked uncertainly. "Is Bardian the oldest son? Will he be head of your family when your uncle is dead? I never wanted to do you harm, Theo."

"You did right, Phano," he assured me at once. His voice was solemn. "You did exactly right. Bardian is a difficult man. He does not care for me, and never has. It's true, I don't go out of my way to make him angry, but I seldom agree with him about anything. Perhaps he does not know how strongly I oppose many of his beliefs. I have kept silent often, when I might have spoken. To say anything, though, would not alter Uncle Bardian's convictions by an iota. You put me to shame, Phano. It's not a feeling I experience frequently." He was silent again. "I have a gift for you, but it is a gift for a child, I am afraid, and you have shown me clearly that you are no child. Perhaps I should not give you my gift."

I laughed. "I have not been given so many gifts that I will reject one without seeing it," I assured him. "Let alone one from you!" I felt the hot blush in my face.

"Look for me tomorrow morning, then, if that is acceptable to your parents," he said.

# ten

"Well done, Phano." Mama laughed. "I could not have stood up more bravely myself. A gift? Now, what might that be? A pair of earrings, perhaps? Or an ornament for your hair?"

Theo had said it was a gift more suitable for a child, so Mama's guesses were almost certainly wrong. I felt very tired, but Theo seemed pleased, not angry, as I had feared he might be, so that was all right. The gift, whatever it might be, would soon be revealed.

We might all have guessed for many hours without hitting the mark. When Theo swung back his cloak next day, he revealed a bundle of something cradled against his chest. He set down the bundle tenderly on a little table. It was perhaps as long and as wide as my thigh shield, though thicker. Was this another thigh shield? No, that was not a gift for a child.

"Help me unwrap it, Phano," he said. "Very carefully, if you please." He kept his big hands near the bundle, as if he feared that I would let it slip off the table.

I unwound long pieces of flannel. At first I was puzzled, but as the oval shape began to emerge, and I felt the slightly rough texture of the creamy white shell, I knew: "It's an egg!" It was indeed an egg, almost too big to cup in my hands. "What kind?"

"A goose egg," said Theo.

"Shall I have it for breakfast, then? It's too big!"

"Thirty days ago, the goose laid that egg. It is due to hatch today. Is it a good gift, Phano? Maybe you don't want a pet at all—or maybe you'd rather have a kitten or a dog."

"No, a goose makes a fine pet."

"If you are there when it hatches, the chick follows you, at least that's what they tell me. Geese live a long time, twenty years or more. So do monkeys, I believe. I wondered about getting you a monkey—but then I saw the geese on your earrings, and that settled it."

"Monkeys bite, the nasty-tempered things. No, thank you."

Theo laughed. "My sisters have one. Bardian's younger brother brought it back from one of his voyages. It does like to nip, but you must not say so, not if you want to be their friend, as I hope you do. A goose can be bad-tempered too, but not to its mistress who saw it come out of the egg. I'm glad I chose the goose. But you see why I said it is a gift for a child."

"It is a wonderful gift, Theo. Am I right, will my goose guard me?"

"Of course it will. A goose often makes a better guard than a dog. Not that I believe you are in danger—but the safer you are, the better contented I will be."

Mama sometimes tells a story about a goose that bit off her friend's little finger when they were slave girls together in Corinth, being raised as courtesans. She learned to do tricks with her four-fingered hand. Later, it helped her to attract clients, because it made her different. As Mama tells it, the tale is very funny, but I was not tempted to tell it to Theo. Dear man.

About that time, we heard the first little tapping noises from the shell. I had watched hens' eggs when they hatched, and had laughed at the wet, bedraggled little chicks. How quickly they dried and turned to fluffy gold, as bright as Theo's hair. My little goose took longer. I was pleased, as Theo and I had a chance to talk, with nothing on our minds except enjoyment of the moment while we waited for something new.

That's what I called my goose, Newby, a bit like New Baby, but different. A goose chick, a gosling, is not a baby. Theo moved away when the egg began to crack open at last. "Your goose must see *you*, and no one else," he said.

"Do I put it on the floor when it's dry?" I asked.

"Yes, and let it follow you around," he replied. "You

must feed it and give it water, and go on letting it follow you."

Newby was a comical baby. I was a giant beside that little ball of fluff, but she was convinced I was her mother. Of course we did not know then if Newby was a goose or a gander, but I said "she." Occasionally, I must admit, she was a nuisance. She hated to be locked up, and she hissed at Father's callers and tried to bite them when they came too close. However, Newby quickly became my loyal companion and my devoted guard.

When Theo gave Newby to me, he told me that the safer I was, the happier he would be. Clearly, I was important to him. As a little sister, or as his future wife? "As his wife, silly," Mama told me. "He'll speak to your father any day now, trust me. He could send someone to speak for him, but I expect Theo will come himself."

On such matters, I trusted Mama more than anybody else. Was she right? I had sometimes dreamed of Theo as my husband, but as a lovely fantasy rather than something that might come to pass.

Could I make Theo a good wife? I had thought that household skills were the only education needed by an Athenian citizen wife; now it was obvious that the King Archon needed a diplomat by his side. No doubt some official qualifications would be required as well. Theo had had to satisfy his examiners that he was a citizen, accepted by his clan, had fulfilled his duties to his parents, I did not know what else. Once more, I thanked the gods that Phrynion's attack on me had not succeeded.

Theo no longer came to our home on business. He had his rooms and his staff near the agora. Father went there as well. When Theo came formally to call on my father, it seemed to be the next step in a pattern. I trembled nonetheless. If he did intend marriage, this was a step closer to reality.

It felt unreal, though. "I wish to marry Phano," Theo said, looking at my father.

Father spoke to me. "Daughter, you would not usually be present when two families met to discuss marriage. As Theo is well aware, however, you have not been raised in ignorance. Theo also wishes to speak to you directly. I have given him permission to do so."

"I hate to bring up bad memories," said Theo, "but I remember our first conversations. Your words stung me then; I remember them now. Phano, our ages are the usual, according to our customs in Athens. I will be thirty-one years old next birthday; you will soon be fifteen. Do I seem very old to you? I want you to be my wife, my *willing* wife." He broke off and looked at me, perplexed.

"As Phano's father, I welcome this match," said Father.

"As Phano's stepmother, I welcome this match," said Mama.

They all looked anxiously at me. The absurdity of the situation struck me, and I burst out laughing. "It appears you are all asking *me!*" I exclaimed. "Well then, as the bride-to-be, if all goes well, I welcome this match."

Everybody laughed, and Minta brought in a jug of the best wine, from Samnos, for a libation. Father asked for the blessing of Father Zeus and Mother Hera on this marriage. Theo asked for the blessing of Athene. Mama said maybe it was not too early to ask the goddess Eileithia to ease the birth of our first child.

"Mama, it is definitely too early for that," I informed her. Then I had to raise the question that was troubling me. "You know my background, Theo." I plunged in. "Will your family accept me?"

"You do go straight to the hard questions." Theo faced me. "My family..." He hesitated, then started over. "Almost all the members of my family agree, especially Uncle Nikos." Theo smiled, as if recalling his uncle's words. Later, he repeated them to me: "If I were fifty years younger, Theo, I'd do my utmost to marry her myself."

Theo continued, "I believe it can be arranged. A good dowry will help, of course." He smiled at Father.

"A good dowry?" I asked.

"No more than usual," said Theo quickly. "Enough so that the interest will maintain you and your servants," he added. "I know you talked of more, Stephanos, but I don't think it's needed. Surely four hundred drachmas a year will keep Phano in style. Interest rates are high at present, but if our party has its way, we'll bring them down. Even so, I doubt they'll fall lower than ten percent. Four thousand drachmas should do it. If it's a little less, nobody will complain." I stood there with my mouth open. Four thousand drachmas? Mama and I did not take part in the great festival of Thesmophoria last fall because we lacked money for the piglets and the priestesses. Four thousand drachmas! But Theo was still talking.

"If you can manage six thousand drachmas, of course, I would not refuse it. An archon's expenses are enormous—I would not have believed how much my office costs. Sacrificial victims—a heifer, ram or goat every second day, it seems, and this one must be pure white, and that one must be black—it drives the price up, I can tell you. Phano's expenses as my wife will be high as well, though they'll go down again when our term is over."

"Father," I began, but both Father and Mama spoke at once, telling Theo my dowry would be arranged, he could be sure of it. Father made faces at me behind Theo's back, and Mama put her fingers on her lips. Well, I might keep quiet for the moment, but they had better be able to explain what magic was going to produce a sudden fortune for me.

"Be happy, Phano," Mama said softly. "We are happy for you, you may be sure."

I wanted to be happy. I wanted to listen to Theo without wondering what Father was up to. It was impossible. Father had borrowed from his own family to buy his office. He could hardly have repaid that loan so soon. Did he have some new plan to "borrow" from the treasury of Athens? What disaster was in the making now?

Theo plowed ahead. He did not notice my distraction.

He saw nothing of the glances and signals that were flying all around him. I saw at once that he would never be a consummate politician. He was too much a man of principle, and trusted too much that others were like him. He would need me to keep him from some fatal misstep. I loved him the more, seeing that he would need my protection, just as I, in other ways, would need his.

"Now that I know how you feel, I want to move ahead quickly," Theo said. "Your father and I will meet Uncle Nikos tomorrow at his home. Please come with us, Phano, my mother will be there; she wants to know you. My grandmother did not attend Bouly's party, and she hopes to meet you too."

"An inspection?"

"No, a visit, that's all, to get to know you better."

He left soon afterward. Father tried to leave with him, but I caught his sleeve and held him back. "Where is this dowry coming from?" I demanded. "Your cousins lent you money to buy your office as assessor. Have you repaid them so soon, that they are ready to put up more money now?"

Father glared at me. His face was red. "There are times when I regret raising you to speak your mind," he snapped. "You lack respect."

"I respect what is respectable," I snapped back.

"Then respect this. It is family money," said Father. "It properly belongs to you, and that is all you are to know." He pulled his sleeve away from my hand and stalked out of the room. I sometimes forget how big Father can be when he is angry. He swells with it. He fills the room.

Mama was no more helpful. "You wanted a respectable marriage, Phano. There will never be a better one. I like it for myself too, if that matters to you. I did not use to be afraid of Phrynion, but every limping step I take is a reminder that he is powerful and my enemy. As Basilinna, you will be beyond his reach; as part of your family, I too will be safe. I do not like myself, being afraid."

"Mama!" Mama had never been afraid, never. Perhaps I was wrong, but if she had been afraid, she had never shown it. Poor Mama! I began to cry, knowing how much she must have hated to admit her fear. If I had been more thoughtful, she could have kept her pride.

Minta gave me one of her mysterious, I-know-more-than-I'm-telling looks when I asked her later about my sudden expectation of wealth in the form of a dowry. "Even if I could guess," she told me, "I am forbidden. Don't worry, Phano, that's all I can say."

I slapped her face, furious that she knew, or pretended to know, something I did not. Minta burst into tears, and I had to comfort her, but I went to bed no wiser than before.

# eleven

The sun roused me from a restless sleep, but my head felt clear. My life had never been untroubled. Why should it be smooth sailing now? I would go forward, as I had in the past, thinking and acting as well as I could, and trusting the goddess to keep me in her care. Mama was right, there would never be a better marriage.

I dressed simply, in a white chiton that billowed out, hiding the narrow gold rope that belted it at my waist. Again Minta helped to dress my hair, pulling it back from my face through a circlet of white wool bound with gold, and twisting my black curls into ringlets. Mama offered rouge for my lips and cheeks, but I refused. Newby followed close on my heels, making little "aw-aw" noises, as she always did when she was excited.

"Newby, you can't come," I told her. "Stay home with Minta, there's a good goose." We had made a leash for Newby, with an embroidered collar round her neck. She was not yet full grown, but she was already strong enough to make it an effort for me or Minta to hold her back.

The late summer sun was hot on our backs as we walked to Uncle Nikos's house. He too had a gatehouse, where a maidservant waited. She led us into the courtyard. It was smaller than Bouly's, or maybe it only seemed smaller, since it was full of flowerbeds ablaze with bloom. One giant oak tree offered shade. Somewhere I could hear water, a fountain perhaps, or a small waterfall. There were herb gardens too, I could smell them. Minta might have found all the herbs for Mama's poultices and sleeping drafts right here. Some poppies still bloomed, though most stems ended in cup-shaped seedpods. The gods be thanked, Mama had survived Phrynion's savage attack.

I snapped back to the present, and to this lovely place. Stone-lined paths curved among the flowers; stools and benches were grouped here and there, beckoning us to take a seat. I loved Father's little house by the Whispering Herm, but sometimes I wished we had a courtyard where we could sit quietly outdoors in the sun.

This visit did feel like an inspection, even though I was sure Uncle Nikos liked me; and I liked him as well. Doors of several rooms off the courtyard stood wide open; the maid showed us into one of them. The old man's chair was placed to catch the sunlight. He looked as if he had fallen asleep. The arms of his chair were carved in the shape of lions' claws, with actual claws set into the dark wood.

One of Uncle's skinny arms lay along one of the chair arms. His fingernails looked like an extra set of talons. He stirred, and his tortoise head leaned forward. Whatever color his eyes had been, they were faded now pale gray-blue, but sharp, not dull or rheumy. He did not pause for pleasantries, but started talking to me as if no time had gone by since Bouly's party, as if he were merely continuing our conversation. "Phano, we must talk more; I think we have much in common—but not today, my dear. Today my time and energy are needed for a different purpose, one that concerns you, as you know.

"Theo, take Phano to your mother, then come back here, my boy." He waved us toward the door. "Now, Stephanos, let's talk about Phano's dowry." If I had thought that a good marriage for me would be possible without a dowry, I thought so no longer. Whatever Father was doing, it needed to be done.

Theo's mother, Isidora—"Call me Dora, Phano dear"—held out both hands to welcome me. She was a comfortable woman, round as an apple, and with cheeks as red. She wore a ring on each plump finger of each small hand. "My husband's mother wants to meet you," she said. "She may have forgotten all about that, however. She may have fallen asleep. Are you used to old people, Phano?"

I had to admit that I was not.

"She lives with us. She sleeps most of the time, but she has her notions, and then we do what she wants. We'll go to her now, I think, better now than later. She is the oldest living member of our family, eighty-six years old next birthday. Isn't that amazing? We're proud of her. As much as possible, we try to let her have her way, though it's a worry when she wants to go visiting. Don't be surprised if she falls asleep."

Theo's grandmother was awake. The whites of her eyes were more yellow than white, and cobwebbed with red veins, but her blue irises were bright and sparkling. I was surprised, having expected her eyes to be faded like her brother's. However, she didn't look much like Uncle Nikos in any way that I could discern.

She eyed me warily. Her white hair was drawn back and twisted into a plain bun, low on her neck. The skin of her face looked thin and soft, like well-worn linen. Folds of skin hung on her neck, for all the world like the wattles of some ancient bird. She wore a dark tunic, and a blanket was tucked around her, though the room was warm.

"Who is this pretty girl?" she asked.

"This is Phano," Dora replied. "You wanted to meet her. You remember, she is going to marry Theo. You know, your grandson Theo."

Dora turned to me. "Sometimes she remembers everything, sometimes not," she said.

"I heard that," snapped the old woman. "There's nothing wrong with my memory, Dora; I'll thank you not to pretend there is. I know I wanted to meet this girl. Don't accuse me of forgetting it. You are Stephanos's daughter, isn't that right?"

"Yes, Grandmother," I said. I hoped she would know that I called her Grandmother, as I might another old lady, in respect, not in expectation.

"Grandmother? I know your grandmother," the sharp voice replied. "Another pretty girl, though I haven't seen her recently. Nobody comes to visit me. When you marry Theo, I'll be your grandmother, won't I?"

Had I heard her right? I looked at Theo's mother, hoping for a clue, but she only shrugged. To my knowledge, no grandmother of mine was living; certainly no grandmother of mine was a pretty girl! Dora had said the old woman was forgetful; probably she lived less in the present than the past. Her head drooped.

"Give her a moment," said Dora. "She'll wake up again."

I did not know what to say. Father rarely spoke of his parents, and never of my true mother's parents. I had used the ivory bobbin to finish weaving the blanket his mother had begun. Father covered himself with it every night, but we had not talked more about his parents, nor were we likely to do so, even if he had not spent most of his waking hours at work with Theo. Any tale this old lady told might be nothing but fantasy, but I would listen eagerly as long as she would talk. The blue eyes blinked open again.

"Please tell me about my grandmother."

"I'll do better than that. Lift your skirts, girl, let's see your ankles. Don't look so shocked, I'm not telling you to take off your clothes." She cackled. "Dora, look at that! Are you proud of them, girl?"

I was proud of my slim ankles, and told her so.

"Your grandmother's ankles, to the life! Ah, she was a lovely girl. She ran like Atalanta, her own grandmother used to say, none of the girls could ever catch her. Are you a runner too?"

I had to admit that I was not. "Pity," she commented; then suddenly her eyes closed again and her head drooped. She blinked and roused for a moment. "I knew your old grandmother too. Long, long ago. I knew them all, but they died." Tears formed in her red-veined eyes and slipped down her waxen cheeks. What did she mean? Was she telling me she had known *both* my grand-mothers?

"My father's mother? You knew her? I use her loom."

The ancient woman closed her eyes. "Go away," she said. "Go, and leave me in peace." Her head drooped. In a moment, she began to snore. I stared at her helplessly.

"That went well, considering everything," said Dora. "She likes you, I can tell. Go now, Phano, you'll have other chances to talk. I'll settle her, then I'll come down."

"Did you hear what I heard, or was I dreaming? What was that about my grandmother and my ankles, and my 'old' grandmother as well?" I asked as soon as Dora came downstairs, but Dora couldn't, or wouldn't, say. She was happy to talk about Theo's childhood, however, and the rest of our visit passed with her recital of his exploits.

Collecting birds' nests, complete with eggs, seemed to have been his favorite pastime. He broke his leg in a fall after he had climbed to a vulture's nest at the top of a cliff.

That was one nest he could not carry home! Two baby birds occupied it, Dora told me. The parents dove at the boy as he climbed down the perilous cliff, throwing him off balance. Knowing Theo now, I would not have guessed he had been so adventurous. It showed a new side of his character. I was grateful.

"I have not bored you? You must truly care for him. Come again when you can. Every mother is full of stories for an eager listener." Dora was amused, and we parted, apparently both well pleased.

# twelve

Soon everything was settled, and our wedding day was named. In less than a month, Theo and I would be husband and wife!

Now all the rituals had to be completed. Most important was my sacrifice to Athene on the Acropolis. The great statue of Athene ranks high among the wonders of the world, so say travelers who have journeyed to the most distant countries, farther than Egypt, farther than ancient Troy. Phidias, who made it, was the greatest sculptor Athens has ever known. I had seen him at work on that very image, in my dream.

The statue stands at the far end of the Parthenon, which is the temple of Athene Parthenos, the Virgin

Athene, born from the forehead of her father Zeus, king of the gods. That is why Athene is so wise, because she was born from her father's forehead. One hundred young girls work together to weave her peplos, a new one every year. She wears the ancient women's dress, with shoulder pins long enough to kill.

Athene is dear to me as the goddess of weaving, and I made my prayer to her in that aspect. "Athene, goddess of weavers," I prayed, "weave my fate and Theo's together, if you are willing, into a perfect fabric." I cut a lock from my hair and laid it reverently at her feet.

The face of the statue looked as the goddess herself must surely look, full of dignity and power. I waited, in case she gave me some sign, but there was nothing, except the sighing of the wind and a little bird crying from the great roof, high above.

My own spinning and weaving had been neglected for some months, in the press of other activities. My bridal chest, however, had been well filled years before. My new household would thank me for a goodly supply of blankets and woven fabrics, some thick and warm for winter garments, others fine and delicate for summer wear. I was especially proud of three scenes I had woven to hang on the walls: Icarus flying toward the sun, Atalanta bending to pick up the third golden apple, and Trojan Hector in his tall war helmet comforting his wife and baby son.

Amid all the wedding preparations, however, I found time to finish the piece on my loom and to sew it into a new cloak for Uncle Nikos. My thigh shield came out of its wrappings often, as I set myself to finish spinning a supply of yarn. Every time I took it out, I glanced at my ankles, and thought about my grandmother, who had rested this shield on her leg, and whose ankles were just like my own, if Theo's ancient grandmother could be believed. Could she really have known both my grandmothers? Was it possible? No matter, soon I would be part of her family. Meanwhile, I chose to believe her.

According to custom, Theo slept at my father's home the night before our marriage. One of Bouly's little brothers was his good-luck child. They arrived together at dusk. Our house was full to bursting with my dowry goods and the supplies for the wedding feast, food, jars of wine, clothes and all manner of other things, but we had cleared out Father's room on the ground floor to make a space for them. We were fortunate; several children in Theo's family had both parents living; he had a choice of good-luck boys. Indeed, three of them were part of our wedding ceremony, crowned with wreaths of thorns and acorns, giving bread to everybody from their little baskets shaped like babies' cradles.

My day began with the bride's ritual bath. Other slaves carried the water that day, but Minta supervised everything. The women assembled: Mama; Theo's mother, Dora; Bouly's mother; Bouly herself; Bardian's wife, Nerissa, too, as fat and piggish as her husband, we couldn't leave her out. All of them took turns scrubbing and wishing me happiness and many children; there was plenty of teasing as well. Nerissa jabbed my thigh with her brush. Looking at her, I could see she had done it on purpose. It hurt, but I just smiled, and Dora picked up the brush.

Then Minta brought my crown and veil for everyone to admire. She had picked the flowers herself that morning and woven them into a circlet, yellow like the sun. My veil was sheerest linen; Dora said she had never seen such fine weaving. All the others agreed, including Nerissa, though she sniffed when she said so.

When everybody was satisfied, Mama took me off to get dressed. My bride's dress was red, according to custom. Some people say, "Happy the bride the sun shines on." Others say rain is a sure sign the marriage will be fruitful. If the omens are good either way, I'd rather have sun.

Phoebus Apollo must have heard my prayer. For Theo and me, the autumn sun shone gold in a cloudless, deep blue sky. That was a relief. We had planned to hold our wedding feast outdoors, in the public garden on the other side of the Whispering Herm. If all the guests had had to squeeze into Father's little house, nobody could have lifted an elbow to carry food to their mouths!

The feast began toward noon. I had not expected Mama to contribute much to it. To my surprise, however, she had gone out to visit everybody she knew who owned a family farm. The harvests had been outstanding. Thanks to Mama's industry, our tables were loaded with purple and green cabbages, olives and sweet onions, along with apples, figs and pomegranates, huge mounds of purple grapes and great rounds of yellow cheese.

The fragrant odor of fresh bread drew me close; I broke off a morsel and dipped it in olive oil, determined to be dainty in my eating, even under my veil. Now that the wedding had actually begun, the appetite that had deserted me the day before had returned; my empty stomach rumbled. I had sent meat and fowl to the bakery to be roasted the night before; we had no way in the house of cooking so much. Minta had supervised the making of hundreds of sweetmeats, little honey cakes stuffed with figs and almonds, apple cakes, cream cakes and others I did not recognize. The wine was well watered, as nobody wanted this wedding to turn rowdy; but the drink was rich and full flavored, and servants kept filling our cups.

As I had hoped, my veil allowed me to observe everything, though it hid my face, as it was supposed to do. Father sat on my right side, Isidora on my left. Theo sat across from me, with Uncle Nikos on one side and Mama on the other. I had hoped to see Theo's grandmother, if only for a short time, but was not surprised when she did not appear. I made a mental note to ask after her later.

The only blight on the day was provided by Bardian. We had had to give him a place of honor, near Theo, and he took advantage of it to glare at Father and me, separately and together, when he was not scouring food from his plate and shoveling it into his mouth. Aunt Pig-Woman sat beside him and glared and shoveled too. I stuck my tongue out at her once, but only once, realizing that the veil might not hide my face completely from her prying eyes.

Nothing could spoil my wedding feast, however, not even Bardian. He was not the Goddess of Discord, who threw a golden apple among the guests at another wedding feast and started the Trojan War. In another hour I would be wife of the King Archon of Athens. Bardian could not harm me.

Father rose at last, to signal the end of the feast. Now came the ceremony itself. My fingers trembled as I untied my maiden's girdle, the wide belt I had worn since my monthly cycles began. "I dedicate this belt, the symbol of my maidenhood, to Artemis," I said. "I thank the goddess of maidens, who has watched over me."

A priestess of Artemis, a white-haired woman in a long silvery blue cloak, came forward to receive my old belt, and to hand me the new one, made specially for this occasion. I had woven it myself, red like my dress, with gold threads running through. Minta had embroidered it with golden acorns. "May you have as many children as these acorns," she had wished. Solemnly, the old priestess bent her silvery head. Each hand grasped one end of my long belt. The bride's belt is always tied with the knot of Hercules, hard enough to tie, but easy to undo. The old woman's hands at my waist moved slowly. Theo would untie that knot, my husband. I felt warm at the thought.

Father's part was next. He lifted the veil from my face and folded it back over my coronet of flowers, smiling tenderly. "Step forward, bride, and meet your bridegroom," he said.

I moved to Theo's side. From that moment, I had no

eyes for anyone else, no thoughts except of us, together. That is as it should be. I committed myself and my happiness to my husband; he received me as his wife.

The sun was still warm on our backs, but our shadows had grown long when at last my new husband seized both my hands and drew me to him. "Come, Wife," he said lightly. "Time to go home."

*How strange!* I thought. *I have lived in other houses, but my father's house is the only* home *I have known, and it will never be my home again.*

Theo might have brought a cart and oxen to lead our procession, but outside the door his chariot waited, drawn by Ajax and Nestor, the two black horses he loved, though not as he loved me. "I am impatient to have you home," he told me.

I looked down like a modest woman in public, but I was as eager as he. My dowry goods would follow us tomorrow. The horses' manes were braided with silver and the harness jingled as Theo stepped up behind me. His body pressed against mine, not modestly at all. Already I was thankful for Mama's teaching, and not shocked at his behavior. He had just taken the reins when there was a flapping and hissing at my feet. Newby!

The guests roared with laughter. "Let her lead the procession," somebody shouted. "She can pull the chariot!" I had penned Newby myself that morning. Who would have let her out?

Bouly covered her mouth with her hand to hide her giggles. "I'll get you for this, Bouly," I hissed, "just you wait." Newby was determined to push Theo off the chariot. She had the element of surprise on her side. Theo recovered his balance quickly, though, and I let Newby stand beside me in front of him. She leaned against me happily.

"Fool that I was, giving you that goose!" Theo grumbled, but there was laughter in his voice. Bouly's giggles were catching, I could not help myself. Besides, everybody knows that a goose is a symbol of good luck. "Giggle as much as you like," said Theo, starting to giggle himself, "but hear me, Wife! That goose stays out of our room tonight. There isn't room for three of us."

"I hear you and obey." I could hardly speak for laughing.

Nothing else delayed us. The horses trotted briskly. Theo halted a time or two to let our friends and families catch up, but we were first to reach the gatehouse. The gate swung wide and we drove through, into the courtyard of my new home.

Slaves and household servants ran to surround us, children as well. Minta laughed up at me; I was happy to see one face I knew. They raised their hands. I knew what was coming, and turned my face to Theo's chest. The shower of nuts and small fruit went on and on. Newby hissed until an apple hit her, then hid her head in my clothes. When I peeked, the women's aprons were still full; the men held bags. This must be the best shower in the world.

The shouts of welcome added to my joy. "May you

be fruitful, Mistress." "May you bear many sons for this family."

*Daughters too,* I thought, *I want Theo's daughters as well as his sons.*

Theo lifted me down. My dress was damp from the servants' welcome. If the grapes and plums left their mark, however, the stains would hardly show. A red dress is practical for a bride.

I looked around. Doors and unshuttered windows in front of us were partly hidden by the wide stairs angling up to the second story. I turned for a quick look around the courtyard, closed in by the four walls of the house. "Big," I muttered. It was bigger than Phrynion's house, bigger than Uncle Nikos's house too. Theo must be richer than I had thought. Was I supposed to manage all of this?

"Don't worry, love." Theo seemed to know my thoughts, not for the first time. "You will manage very well. This is your talent, Phano, my wife."

The servants parted for Theo's mother, that brisk little dumpling of a woman who had sat beside me at the feast. She smiled at us, loving and comfortable, and reached for my hand. "Come, Daughter."

She led me to the hearth, where she made a sacrifice to the goddess Hestia, welcoming me to my new family. Then I followed her up the wide stairs.

Daughter, she called me.

For months, I had dreamed of being married to Theo. I had spent hour after hour planning to be his perfect wife. For months, I had watched him and learned. He liked his stew hot, his bread pulled brown from the fire, his goats' cheese soft, his wine well watered. As to the cheese, that would depend on the goats and on the season: the rest I could manage. More than most people, Theo liked clean clothes and clean feet. I had never been near him when he did not smell clean. I would have loved him stinking of sweat if I had to, but clean is easier.

In this house, the slave girls would continue to bring water for Theo's bath, but now I would have charge of his laundry. I would examine every garment after it had been washed. I knew what I'd say if there was a mark, even a little one: "Look, girl, there's a stain on your master's tunic. Heat fresh water and scrub it properly—and be more careful in future. If I find a spot again, your back will smart for it!"

I had prepared myself to be a wife.

I knew that Theo's family would be my family when I married him. Mama often said she had no family but Stephanos and me. That's because his relatives did not want anything to do with her, it's not because her family were all dead, even though they were. Now Mama didn't have me either. She was still my stepmother, who had raised me as her own, nothing could change that, but I would be a daughter in this family now. My breath caught in my throat as we came to the top of the stairs and entered the women's room, where my looms already waited. One of the doors ahead would lead to the room Theo and I would share.

"Mother," I gulped.

She turned at once. "Well, Daughter?" She smiled again. "It seems strange to me too, Phano. I never had a grown-up daughter until today. We'll know better as the days go by, but I can see you're a sensible girl, modest— you know how to behave in company. Anyone can tell that you care for your husband, and he for you. Like as not, we'll do well together." She laughed merrily. "You can teach *me* a thing or two about spinning, from the look of it—where by rights I should be teaching *you!*"

I was going to ask if she would permit me to visit Mama and Father whenever I wanted, but I changed my mind. Isidora—Dora—was my mother now.

She swung back a heavy door. Iron hinges creaked, and I reminded myself to silence them with oil. "Your room," she said, "yours and Theo's, of course."

*Too big,* I thought, *and the wide bed, too big.* Had it been her room before her husband died? Theo was her only son, we should have the best room, it was only right. Moonlight streamed in through a big window. I looked out, and saw the inner courtyard below.

"Has your stepmother prepared you for your wedding night?" my new mother asked. "Is there anything you would like to ask me?"

"No, thank you, Mother." What a question! Did she know nothing about Nera, this new mother of mine? What would she say if she heard I had spent part of my childhood in houses whose business was the pleasures of men? If I had been ignorant, Phrynion's threats had left nothing to the imagination. He had told me exactly what he planned. Mama had given me herbs and potions to help make a baby or prevent one, paying no attention when I told her I wanted all Theo's babies, as many as I could have.

Dora was the kind of Athenian wife I wanted to be, if I could forget what I knew. So she thought I could teach her a thing or two about spinning, did she? No help for it, a laugh burst out of my throat. I turned it into a kind of snort. Maybe she'd take it for a sneeze.

"Prickly, are you? My question was well meant."

"So kind," I babbled.

"Maybe. Theo is a good man. He will be a faithful husband, Phano. I trust you to be a loving and loyal wife. I'll send him to you." She left. Her back was stiffer than when she entered. Not a perfect start.

The perfect start came later, with Theo. "I wanted to be the first to undo your woman's girdle," he told me.

"My husband, you are the first."

❀

When Odysseus came home to his own wide bed and his dear wife, Penelope, after twenty years, Athene held back the chariot of the sun. Alas, my husband and I had no goddess to do the same. The sky was already lightening toward dawn when we fell asleep with our arms around each other.

Happy days, and happy, happy nights. They did not last. Our lives were carefree for a few short days, no more. Then the family held a quiet funeral for Theo's grandmother, who had been closer to death than anyone realized. I would have been part of the women's group who stood around her body and followed in procession to her grave, but I was feverish and Mother sent me to bed.

"Grandmother was so old," said Theo, "her death is not really a surprise, except that it *is* a surprise, if that makes any sense. I know she was young once, if I think about it, but for me she was always old, even when I was a boy. I just didn't think she would die. I thought she'd go on forever. I do know better." He looked at me ruefully.

I felt as rueful as Theo looked. Whatever his grandmother had known about my family, I would never have more than that single tantalizing glimpse of it. "I am sorry for your loss," I told Dora and Theo, and it was true, but I was sorrier for my own. Then Theo's duties as Basileus took over his life, and mine as Basilinna took over mine.

Less than two weeks after our wedding, Theo had to go to Delos, the sacred island. In past ages, the treasury was kept on Delos. Now it remains in Athens, but the Basileus must make the journey from time to time. We were in bed when he told me, warm and loving. I burst into tears. Theo wrapped his arms around me and hugged me so tight I could hear my ribs crack. "Poor baby," he murmured. "Poor little girl."

I stopped in midsniffle. "I am not poor. I am not little. I am not a child." Nera herself could not have put more outrage into her voice. I sat up and pulled the coverlet around me. "I am your wife, Theo, and I will miss you. That's all."

He roared with laughter.

113

"You did that on purpose!" I almost slapped his face, but I tickled him instead, under his arms and on the soles of his feet, and he tickled me back in various interesting places.

Later, when we had slept for a few hours and wakened, I asked about the journey. I wanted to know everything about Theo's business, even if that was not the usual way of an Athenian wife. I am not stupid. Theo said I helped him, sometimes with my ideas, sometimes just by listening to him. That's the way I was brought up. A woman must keep quiet about it, of course. When her husband trusts her with his secrets, she must keep them safe. Mama did not always mind her tongue. Father complained about it once. "My friends make fun of me," he told her. "Like Pericles, hiding behind a woman's skirts."

"Don't let cheap comments trouble you," Mama replied. "Who is better remembered in Athens today, the courtesan Aspasia or the hero Pericles?" Father had no reply.

Mama was right. Pericles built the Parthenon. Pericles commissioned the wondrous statue of Athene. Pericles rebuilt the long walls from the harbor to the city. Pericles made Athens rich. Athens will remember Pericles forever. Aspasia was his partner in all of it, but many people today don't even know her name. Perhaps Mama talked so confidently because she ate with the men, always at our home, and sometimes in public too.

At my new home, the women ate with the men too. "I thought perhaps we women would eat by ourselves," I told Dora.

"Are you shy?" she asked. "We are not a big group in this house; we like to be together at family meals. When Theo entertains other archons, or officials on his staff, or emissaries from another city, Sparta, or Corinth, or Thebes, perhaps, or the island of Delos, or when he invites his friends to a symposium, naturally we women dine upstairs."

"I am not shy," I told her.

"I did not think you were," she said.

If I had been shy, my public role as Theo's wife would have been difficult. Even as a child, I loved the fun and excitement of a festival, and we have many festivals in Athens, honoring the gods. Oschophoria was the first big festival after my marriage. No, Apaturia was first, but I had no duties there. Oschophoria had long been a favorite of mine. I sat with Theo to watch the procession of young men as they began the footrace to Phaleron. The leaders were dressed like girls, according to custom; they looked very natural, except for the down on their faces, not yet proper beards.

Then Theo went to preside over the wrestling, and I turned toward the theater. Families were already sitting on the banked stone seats, and the grass in front was crowded with little children. The storyteller greeted me, smiling. "This must be my lucky day," he said, "to be introduced by such a lovely Basilinna."

He was famous, but I had not heard him before. In his arms he held a big-bellied lyre, the most beautiful I had seen. Its body was not wood, but polished tortoiseshell. His kind words gave me confidence, and I made my voice loud, presenting him to his audience. That day he told the tale of the hero Theseus, who saved the boys and girls of Athens from being killed and eaten by the Cretan Minotaur.

Like everyone else, I thrilled when Theseus offered himself to go to Crete, laughed when he teased the other victims to cheer them up, and shuddered when he went all alone into the dark labyrinth, unrolling the thread that would lead him out again after he had killed the monster. Like the others, I groaned when Theseus forgot to change his black sail to white on his homeward journey, and wept when his father threw himself from a cliff into the ocean, thinking his son was dead. The tale ended as Theseus became king of Athens in place of his father. The faces round me were filled with pity for Theseus, gaining the kingship so sadly, and with fear of the gods, who can turn joy to sorrow so fast.

# thirteen

In the weeks after our wedding, Uncle Nikos dined with us often. I was always happy to see him. Theo was used to bringing Uncle Nikos home without advance warning to either his mother or me. "That's fine," I assured him. "In this house, we can always feed one more person, especially one with a small appetite. Don't change your ways, Theo, just because you are married."

We looked at each other. Perhaps I blushed. Theo and I had both changed our ways because we were married. Often we said little things to each other that reminded us. I wonder if most new-married couples are as happy as we were? It seems unlikely. We went around smiling at each other, dreaming of each other, like a couple of idiots—or lovers—perhaps there is little difference. When Theo told me he had invited Uncle Bardian and his wife to dine, along with their two grown sons and their unmarried daughter, I was less happy.

"Did you have to? Theo, that man despises me."

"He should have a chance to know you, Wife. How else can he learn better?"

"Six guests for dinner," said Dora. "Uncle Nikos will be here as well, won't he?" Theo nodded. "That's a challenge for a young bride," Dora continued. "May I help?"

"Please tell me what they like to eat," I asked her. "If I am to impress them, I'd like to be able to say I prepared the food myself."

"You might guess the most important thing from their looks," said Dora acidly. "Make three times as much of everything as you would for anybody else, and you'll be right."

I did not tell her I called Bardian Pig-Man. It was lacking in respect.

They arrived together, all six of them, exactly on time. I already knew that Bardian and his wife were as fat as pigs. So were their children. They ate like pigs too, snorting and grunting. I would have hated them even if they had not turned out to be supporting Phrynion. My ears pricked up when I heard that name!

"You made a speech against Phrynion last week in the Agora," said Bardian to Theo. His little eyes were red slits in his porky cheeks. How Uncle Nikos could have fathered such a son is beyond me. If ever a child should have been exposed at birth, that child was Bardian, but I suppose his father could not have known when he was born how badly he would turn out.

I was too angry to listen to the man for the next few sentences, but he was still in full voice when I opened my ears again. "Athens must lower taxes for rich men, Theo. What is the use of ruining men of property so that we cannot trade with other cities, cannot send out ships loaded with olive oil and wine to sell in far places, cannot bring home money and goods to make Athens rich?"

"Do these men make Athens rich, or only themselves?" Theo's voice was cool. I was glad he had said it; otherwise, I would have said it myself.

"They make *us* rich, that counts for something!" said Bardian. "When you oppose Phrynion's low-tax policy, you hurt your whole family, Theo, and every other Athenian with property as well. We all resent it.

"Change your ways, I say. Do you want to bankrupt yourself equipping a fighting ship for the navy, or rebuilding the long walls? Defense costs money, boy, and that means heavy taxes for all of us who have money. Who wants that? The sooner you come over to Phrynion and me, the better."

"Phrynion is a cheat and a liar." They all stared at me with their mouths open. I should have known better. When women eat with men in Athens, they do not talk like men. They do not criticize men, especially men who are powerful and rich.

Bardian glared at me. "Phrynion had a run-in with

119

your mother, didn't he? I'd forgotten about that." I could almost see the little wheels in his mind going click, click, click. "She was his slave, if I remember rightly. Your mother. And what would that make you, aside from a woman who can't bite her tongue?"

Theo jumped to his feet. He gripped his uncle's shoulder. My blood was up as well. Theo's fist felt like *my* fist, poised to hit the pig-man's chins.

"Sit down, Theo. Don't move, Bardian." Great-uncle Nikos's voice was clear and firm. "You shame me, both of you. You also shame the newest member of our family. Phano is the daughter of Athenian parents, both citizens of this city. Her mother was not a slave." He smiled at me. "You dislike Phrynion, young woman. No doubt you have your reasons. It's not always wise to express yourself so strongly, though, or so loudly either. An archon's wife brings credit to her husband when she thinks before she speaks."

I felt crushed. He was right, of course—but how could I have kept quiet? "I'm sorry," I mumbled. Then pride stiffened my backbone. I lifted my head and looked straight at Pig-Man. "I am sorry I offended you, sir. That was not my wish. Phrynion may be a man of honor and principle to you and to your friends, but I have much reason to distrust him. I too speak as a member of this family, though a recent addition, and young, and a woman."

"If you were my wife, I would beat you." Bardian spoke through his teeth. From the look on his wife's face, she would be eager to take her turn with the whip. "No offense, Theo," Bardian added hastily. "Thank you for dinner. We'd best be going."

"Cousin, let's talk again when I return to Athens," said Theo amiably. "We might meet at the Agora, without my little firebrand bride. Not that I completely disagree with her, you know. I fear the threat from the north."

"What threat? Philip of Macedon could die next year, and his armies would melt away. We'd have spent our money for nothing."

"He is young and in health, and stronger every day. When did he seize our Thracian gold mines? Seven years ago? Eight? He made himself rich and us poor at the same time. Now he gobbles up the small cities to the north, and we don't help them.

"Thebes will be next, mark my words, Bardian. Remember our treaty: Athens will have to help Thebes. How can we do anything for our allies if we do not arm? If Thebes is defeated, Philip will be free to throw his full force against us. How shall we defend Athens if the long walls fail and we cannot bring in food, supplies and troops by sea?"

"That's nonsense. Philip respects Athens. He'd rather trade with us than destroy us. You young men all want war. It's a quick way to make your fortunes. You mark *my* words, Theo: it's a quicker way to die. Better to give up some land to Philip, if we must, a northern city or two, enough to keep him quiet, not enough to hurt us here. Better to keep our rich men strong!"

"Bardian, I'll ask you not to talk like that in public," said Uncle Nikos. "If you believe what you've been saying, your mother and I have raised you badly. We have had enough empty mouthing at this table tonight, I'll not add to it. Winter is coming, my bones feel the chill." Uncle Nikos leaned on the edge of the table in front of him, trying to get up. The table trembled. In another moment, he would have been lying on the floor under a mess of stew, wine and cut-up fruit. I started to my feet, but my husband was nearer, and faster.

"Take my arm, Uncle." Theo steadied the old man, and the table, and managed to make his quick movements easy and gracious. Admirable man! "These are hard times for Athens," he said, "when families are divided. We may have different notions of what's best for our city, but we all care for Athens, and for each other. I trust and love every member of my family, never doubt it." He smiled at his great-uncle. He smiled at Pig-Man and Pig-Woman. He smiled at his mother and me. Ten minutes before, I would not have believed it possible, but all of us smiled back.

Late in the night, Bardian's words came back and circled in my mind, nibbling darkly at my happiness. "She was his slave, if I remember rightly. Your mother. And what would that make you?"

So Phrynion was still spreading lies about me, and it seemed that Bardian, who would be head of Theo's clan when Uncle Nikos died, believed him.

Perhaps the Goddess of Discord *had* been present at

our dinner that night. Why else would such a horrid suspicion leap into my mind? Was it possible that Phrynion was right, that Nera was in fact my mother, not my stepmother? The ugly thought had no sooner come to me than other thoughts added weight to it. Why had my mother's family never welcomed me? I knew nothing about them.

What good family would treat a child, even a female child, like that? If I was, as Father had told me, the daughter of two Athenian citizens, properly married to each other, accepted by my father as his own child, why was half of my family missing? Why, unless Father and Mama had both lied to me?

When I was a child, I wished Mama was my mother, not my stepmother. Then I got older and it did not matter. She raised me. Why would she pretend to be my stepmother, if I was truly her own child? In the dark night, the answer leaped out: if the pretense succeeded, life would be better for all three of us.

Mama was a free woman when I was born. She had the rights of a free woman married to an Athenian citizen. My father was certainly an Athenian citizen, but Mama had certainly been a slave. What did that make me? If I was her child, I was not a citizen, not a worthy bride.

Had Father deceived my new family? Would my father do such a thing? I would not have expected him to lie in such a matter, but I had to admit it was not impossible. Father can talk himself into bad actions in hopes of bringing about good results.

Mama would have supported Father; indeed, it might have been her idea. What could be more practical? Mama has been practical about me as long as I can remember.

Everything I had longed for had come true: marriage and a position greater than I had ever hoped; as respectable a family as any in Athens; trust and respect in my home; and love, so much love.

Was it all based on a lie?

# fourteen

Obviously, I needed to talk to Mama, and probably to Father as well. False ideas can grow in a person's mind; the best way to get rid of them is to see and talk to people who know the truth. The more I thought about it, though, the less I wanted to talk to Father about my birth. It would be hard to bear if he lied to me and I found out afterward.

Theo threw an unexpected roadblock in my way. "Dear wife," he said, "please don't invite your mama here at present."

"Why on earth not?"

"She and Stephanos dined at Saurias's home last week. You remember Saurias."

"Saurias." I rolled the name over on my tongue before

I remembered. "He was the umpire in Mama's case. It seems so long ago."

"If your mama had not made Phrynion so angry, I might never have met you. I'd be married to some dough-faced doll." He made a face of disgust. "The gods smiled on us when Phrynion stole you away, though I did not think so at the time.

"Uncle Bardian dined with Saurias that day, as well as Stephanos and Nera. Phrynion was there as well, so they tell me." Theo's eyes twinkled. "State business kept me busy, or I would have been there myself. I'm sorry I missed the fun; it would have been something to remember, all of them together."

"Did one of them start a fight?"

"No, nothing like that, though I don't doubt they came close. No, but Nera was the only wife at the party; the other women were all courtesans."

"You knew she did things like that, Theo. It's not the first time."

"True—but Mother has heard about it for the first time, no doubt from dear Cousin Nerissa. Bardian will have been quick to spread the news, likely with some embroidery in the telling. Mother is upset."

"Why has she not talked to me about it?" But reasons were not hard to find. Perhaps Theo's mother was wondering about me, in the same way I was wondering about my father. Perhaps she was afraid to ask, in case I lied to her, and she found out later. Perhaps there were some things she would rather not know.

Theo put his arms around me. "Mother needs time, dear wife, that's all. She does not know you as well as I do. Her life has been sheltered, but she values strength and integrity, and recognizes them too. She likes you, darling. Give her time, she will love you fiercely. I believe she will accept Nera as well, but this is not the time. You do understand?"

Unhappy as I was, I understood well enough. As usual at a time of tension and worry, I turned to my spinning. The old thigh shield—so big and heavy when I first began to use it—fitted my leg perfectly now. As fall turned to winter, I turned huge piles of carded wool into huge balls of yarn.

The days were short now, but I could spin as well in the half-light as in full day; I worked by touch rather than by sight. The long, dark hours soothed my spirit. Gradually, the turmoil in me receded, and I grew calm again. Why should I question Mama or Father? Whatever the truth might be about my birth, I was Theo's wife. Nothing could change the past. We are all—always—in the hands of the gods.

Dora—Mother—marveled at my skill. She would have chatted, but I was caught up in my own thoughts. I don't talk much when I spin at any time; it spoils the rhythm. Mother seemed abashed when I told her, but she accepted it kindly. Often she sat with me quietly, sometimes taking up her own spindle, sometimes not. I grew accustomed to seeing her out of the corner of my eye, so much that I began to miss her when she was not there.

We did not talk about Mama. I did not invite her to our home and did not see her privately. Naturally, she came with Father from time to time, eating with us as family. Mama did not dress her hair elaborately on these occasions; her makeup was subdued, her clothing of best quality, but plain. Without makeup, her poor nose and lips plainly showed their injuries. Dora was polite but formal; so was Mama. I watched my two mothers wretchedly, but had no power to intervene.

Theo dined more often with other men than with us at home, but he arranged to join the family for a quiet celebration of my fifteenth birthday. Bardian and Nerissa were not invited; Father and Mama were. Mama's limp was worse than it had been. Her hair showed more gray than red. Worse, as the meal progressed, she kept her eyes on her food. Her voice was silent. Where were Mama's light and fire? Seeing her so sadly changed made me want to weep. Father behaved much as usual, laughing and joking with everybody, talking, talking, talking. He was doing an audit of the financial records of the city, tracing them back.

"I wanted to go back ten years," he said, "but it's impossible."

"Why impossible?" I asked.

"Too big a job," said Father. "Such a mess, I would not have believed it. Five years may be possible."

"We need to know how we've spent our money," said Theo. "That will give us a basis for planning. Many people think it's personal, though, that you're hunting for evidence against them. Your work makes them nervous."

"Some of them ought to be nervous," Father replied. "I'm a reasonable man; officials deserve some profit for their hard work during their term of office, that's the way the world goes. Some of them have clearly overstepped the mark, however.

"Just yesterday I checked out a contract for repair work on the oldest part of the Long Wall, not far from the city. Three master masons and a crew of fifty men, half of them free men, were paid for six months' work. I won't say that nothing at all was done, but no more than ten good workers could have finished in a week! That's going too far. And the records are abominable! Nobody really knows where the money has gone. If I do nothing else, Theo, I will leave Athens with a system of record keeping for the future."

"You will make enemies along the way," said Dora. "Take care, Stephanos, you are part of our family now."

"I'm proud of you," I told him. "Mama, this is exactly what you talked about, years ago. You knew how Father could serve Athens best. Do you remember?"

Mama's smile used to be merry. Now, with her twisted lips, it seemed almost sinister.

# fifteen

In Athens, we honor the gods. We are proud of our festivals and of all our rites, greater and lesser. Hardly a day goes by but some small procession wends its way through the city, girls walking to the Delphinion carrying boughs of olive wrapped with wool, or boys following their chorus master on the way to practice their recitations.

The great festivals are very different from these small events. From my wedding day, I had known that the festival of Anthesteria would be crucial for me. The Basilinna's role there is her most important duty, perhaps the most important duty of her life. Even so, it was a shock when the high priestess of Dionysos sent for me, more than two months before the time.

"I have never instructed so young a Basilinna," she grumbled. Her fingers were bent like bows, and bony as Death. Brown liver spots covered her hands. When she opened her mouth, it was easy to see she'd lost almost all her teeth. I knew her breath would stink, but I did not shrink back when she seized my shoulders and stared into my eyes.

"Is the Basileus your first husband?" she demanded. "Were you a virgin when you married him?"

I did not flinch. "He is my first and only husband," I said firmly. "I was a virgin on my wedding day."

"You have courage," the ancient priestess told me. "You will need it, to be the bride of the god."

"What do you mean, Mother?" My assurance wavered.

"You will learn, child," she replied. "First, however, I must be certain that you are fit to know these mysteries, to be initiated at the deepest level. Next, I must be satisfied that you can learn your role and perform your part. On the second day of the Anthesteria, the future of Athens will depend on you. Are you worthy?"

"I hope so, Mother." My back stiffened.

"I hope so as well. There are some doubts, I must tell you. I will question you hard. Believe me, I am not easily deceived. Unless I can be sure of you, girl, your husband must divorce you and take another wife." Hot words rose to my lips, but Uncle Nikos came into my mind at the same instant, reminding me that the Basilinna must guard her tongue.

"The gods do not love pride," I told the old woman. "I will not stand before you and swear by Dionysos that I will be and do everything as you command. Your questions will be answered honestly, that is my promise. I love Athens more than my life. Teach me, Mother, what I must do."

It must have been a good answer. She dropped her hands and stood back. I breathed deeply, in and out. "Sit down." She pointed to a low stool and took another one herself. "Let us begin."

I sat with her for a long time. She questioned and I answered as well as I could. My answers must have gone some way to content her. At length she stopped questioning and began to teach. "There are fourteen altars," she told me, "fourteen priestesses, and you. You must administer a great oath to each priestess: 'I sanctify myself and am pure and holy, from all things that are not purifying, and particularly from intercourse with a man, and I shall act as a reverend priestess now and twice more when I am called upon." It was a long oath; that was no more than the beginning.

"Say it after me," she said; and then, "Say it yourself.

"Again.

"Again.

"Again."

My body ached with weariness when at last she said it was enough. "Repeat these words many times each day," she told me. "You are the youngest Basilinna I have ever seen. It would not astonish me if every word vanished from your mind when the time came, but I tell you now, Phano, on your life, that must not happen. I must be sure of you."

She sent me away with instructions to return in three days. My stomach was tight, so that I could not eat dinner. Somebody had raised doubts about me, somebody had been whispering in the old priestess's ear. What should I do? With Theo's consent or without it, I needed Mama's advice.

That night, like many others, I was asleep when my husband came home. As usual, he rose in the faint predawn light. I was awake, I might have explained matters and told him what I needed, but the moment passed, and he was gone. I took matters into my own hands and sent Minta to bring Mama quietly to me.

It seemed a pity not to go myself to the little house by the Whispering Herm, but I was determined to be cautious. The old priestess had tested me hard. If enemies watched outside the house, they should not see me go to Mama's house, attended only by a slave. If spies watched at home, they should see me at my proper work. The spindle leaped into my hand.

When Minta brought Mama, quietly dressed and veiled, I asked her to stay with us. Minta sniffled and blew her nose. "You have not wanted any advice from me for a long time," she said. "I thought you were through with me, except to dress your hair and run your errands."

Poor Minta! "Not likely," I told her. "You nursed me, Minta. I hope you live to nurse my children."

"By Aphrodite's girdle!" Mama laughed. "So that's why you called me here!" Her eyes slipped down to my belly.

"No, I'm not pregnant," I told her. It was her constant hope, of course, mine too, though Theo and I had been married so short a time. "The goddess has not yet blessed us. Soon, if she is kind. This is something else entirely, and much less happy. The priestess of Dionysos has called me to her to instruct me in the Mysteries of the Anthesteria.

"Mama, did you know that *I* must marry the god, whatever that means? I knew I had to lead the ceremonies of the second day, and they are heavy, but I did not know about the sacred marriage. Mama, everything depends on it. The future of Athens will lie in *my* hands!"

"So?" Hera be thanked, Mama sounded like herself again. Mama was not awed. In times past Mama would not have been awed if Zeus himself came to her, like Danae, in a shower of gold, or if he appeared as a swan, the way he did with Leda. Now she smiled and said, "Athens is in good hands, then. Nobody cares more for her than you, Phano."

"Truly," I agreed. I sat straighter on my four-legged stool. Then my spindle slowed; my yarn suddenly tangled and snapped, as it has scarcely done since I was seven years old and no more than a beginner.

"Tell me about this priestess," Mama urged. "You don't usually behave like this, Phano. What did she say to you?"

"She is so old," I started, then stopped. "Mama, she said I would need courage to be the bride of the god."

"So? You don't lack courage, Phano. I don't know exactly what she meant, but other women have done this, and so can you. There must be more to it, to get you in such a flap. Come, spit it out!"

"She has doubts about me. If I am not worthy, Theo must divorce me and take another wife."

*Are you really my mother, Mama? Did you carry me in your body, as well as your heart?* The words trembled on my lips. I had waited and waited for a chance to ask. Now the chance lay before me, but I did not speak. I stared at her. She stared at me. Tension thrummed between us, taut as the rope that moors a ship in a storm.

"That priestess must be sure of you, then," Mama said at last. "We must remove her doubts, whatever they may be.

"What more do you know about this Mystery, and your part in it? We don't make so much of it in Corinth, not in Megara either."

Mama's calm voice soothed me, as she intended. I picked up my yarn and started to untangle it. "There will be fourteen altars, Mama. Fourteen priestesses, and a great oath." I pronounced the oath, giving each word its full solemn weight.

"You have learned that much already, Mistress," said Minta admiringly. "I could not remember all of it, I'm sure."

"It's a beginning," Mama agreed. "You administer this oath to the fourteen priestesses. What then?"

"I don't know everything," I replied. "The helpers bring the animals for sacrifice, and the knives, for me as well as the others."

"Lambs?"

"Baby lambs." Poor babies, they would never run in the meadows when the sun turned warm. The girls would never pet them and put daisy chains around their soft little necks. Those necks would bow to knives as sharp as Theo's razor. "Oh, Mama, do I *have* to?" But I knew the answer.

"You love babies, Phano. Kittens, puppies, little pigs, geese just hatched, scrawny wet little nothings, all open mouths. You love anything little and weak, you always have."

Geese just hatched! I wanted to race to the courtyard to make sure Newby was safe. My yarn tangled again.

"Put your spinning down, girl," Mama snapped. "You are the Basilinna now. What do you love better, Athens or a few silly little lambs?" Mama could still slap my face harder with a few words than with her hands. Phrynion had dented her spirit, not killed it. I thanked the gods, and pushed my doubts away.

"You know how Macedon threatens us. Athens needs every citizen, every foreigner who lives here, every slave. Thank the gods who have given you a part to play. Your father says Philip of Macedon will march against us, likely inside the next ten years, certainly inside the next twenty."

"Theo says it too." I shook my head. "All the same, Mama: How can fifteen dead lambs keep Philip away?"

"We sacrifice to the gods, that's our duty. They accept the sacrifice and help us. This is something to *do*, not something to think about." Mama's voice was sharp. "I think you need to practice. I'll arrange it."

"No need, I won't hesitate. I wish it was a libation of new wine, instead of blood." I shivered. "Forgive the thought, Lord Dionysos," I added quickly.

Mama made the sign to ward off harm. "The god whom you must marry. What can you tell us about that?" she demanded.

It's fortunate that Mama cannot see all my thoughts. She is uncanny enough. She was right; the "marriage" part was where I needed her help. Often her unconventional life has made my life difficult, as with Dora on my wedding night. On this occasion, her experiences seemed likely to be useful.

"It is truly a mystery." I hesitated. "In part it is a mystery even to the old priestess, who has attended the Basilinna every year since before I was born! The sanctuary in the Marshes is closed up all year, Mama, except for this one day. There will be singers, puppet plays, all kinds of contests—a drinking contest is one of them, with the new wine—little wine jars as gifts for the children. The altars are set up outside, under the sky. After the sacrifice, I make my own vow to be a worthy bride of the god. Then I take my lamp and enter the shrine. The god will meet me there. Later, there will be a great wedding feast.

"It sounds like a wonderful day, Mama. Children are a big part of it. Why on earth did you never take me? It would be so much easier if I had been there, even once or twice." I sighed and told how I had asked the old priestess, "What if it should rain?"

"What did she say?"

" 'Have you never been there? Why not?' Her old eyes burned me; her face was white with anger, all but her eyes. 'I have never known it to rain,' she said when I did

137

not reply. 'We are in the god's hands.' I hope Dionysos looks kindly on me," I added grimly.

Mama seemed to shrink in front of me. "I did not take you because of who I am," she said flatly. "For your own sake, Phano."

"Forgive me, Mama." I put my arms around Mama and hugged her. I drew Minta into our circle and we all three hugged and cried and hugged.

"Minta, you and I will find out what we can," said Mama some time later. "The slaves will talk to you; the courtesans will talk to me." She sounded like herself again, much to my relief.

# sixteen

When I bowed before the old priestess for the second time, she seemed less formidable than before. I repeated my lesson perfectly. "Good," she said. "We will continue. The shrine will be open when you arrive. After the ritual at the altars, you make your own vow, in front of all the people. Then you must enter the shrine. What you are to do there will be revealed at the time, and only to you. No person except the Basilinna may enter that sacred shrine, or experience these Mysteries. It is forbidden to say anything of them to anyone.

"For a person impure or false in thought, to enter these sacred places, to speak these sacred words, to perform these sacred rituals, is sacrilege; and death is the punishment. In the old days, the Queen of Athens entered into the sacred marriage. Now we have no queens in this city, yet on this day, you, Phano, are a queen, and sacred. Time out of mind, it has been so." She lifted her face to the sky, and a light shone from her face, so that she seemed greater than human. "You must swear an oath to Zeus and all the Olympian gods to keep these things close to your heart."

"Mother, do not doubt I will do so." I was exalted, like her, and full of awe.

I knew little more about my marriage to Dionysos when next I saw Mama.

She had talked to a few courtesans. "We know more about men's rituals than women's," she said. "It's natural, when one thinks about it."

"I haven't done any better with my friends," Minta admitted, "though I have not seen many of them yet. Phano, what else did the priestess tell you?"

"Not much," said I. "The god will rise from the Underworld to join his bride.

" 'What then?' I asked her.

" 'What happens after every wedding, to make it complete,' she said. 'Make good your marriage to the god, Basilinna, and everywhere in Attica the grapes will grow fat and full. All the crops will be good. Fail in your duty, and the fruit will wither on the vines, and all creatures miscarry.' "

I sighed.

"That is heavy," said Minta.

"'Help me, Mother,' I begged her. 'Tell me more.' But she would not—or could not—tell me any more."

My hands are always calm; this is why I can win prizes with my spindle. Now, as I re-created the scene, my hands twisted together. My teeth closed on my lips; I tasted blood. "This is too chancy altogether," I told Mama. "The old priestess said it would be difficult for me, and she would know if I had succeeded or not. 'I always know, afterward,' she said.

"I believe her," I added.

"Mama, I know what happened when I married my husband. He was my first man, and I hoped he would be my last. I never asked to marry a god. What can I expect from this marriage?"

"Hmmm." Mama put her hand under her chin and frowned. She looked adorable. I wish I had the trick of it, frowning and looking adorable at the same time. I had been wrong, thinking men would never want to look at her again.

"It may be that the priest takes the place of the god," said Mama thoughtfully.

"I'd hate that. So would Theo." My voice was calm, but inside I shivered.

"So would any husband," Mama agreed. "Now that I think about it, we can be sure that's not the custom here in Athens. In this city, the old families think they're so important!" She sniffed, in infinite scorn.

"If the Basilinna is always the bride, won't her husband take the part of the god?"

"Perhaps," Mama agreed. "A child of the god and a child of the family; a double blessing, what could be more fortunate? Minta, try again. Talk to slaves in other households, last year's Basilinna and a few others. It's lucky you are such a gossip. We don't have much time."

Minta did her best. She brought many rumors and some solid information to our next meeting, but nothing to the point.

"It can't be the Basileus," I said. "Somebody would have talked, or nodded, or winked." Mama and Minta agreed with me at once. That may be a record!

"You will wed a herm, then," said Mama.

"A herm? A little stone man? How can that be?"

"Part of him won't be so little." Minta giggled.

"How can you be so crude? Minta, you'll disgrace me yet." Minta keeps forgetting she's part of a respectable household now.

"Enough," Mama snapped. "It may not be so difficult. This marriage may be no more than talk and pantomime. The ritual will be revealed to you; I don't know how, I don't know what—and you must never tell a living soul, not even your husband. That would be a profanation of the Mystery. It would be danger to Athens, and disgrace, perhaps even death, to you." She stood over me, regal as a goddess herself. "I will take my leave," she announced.

"Minta, see my stepmother to the gate." Why did I not call her Mama? For no reason, except anger, and I had no reason for that. She had helped me. But I did not call after her, using the love name, the child name I had always used.

By bad luck, Theo arrived as Mama was leaving. They met at the gate. Theo did not beat me, but he reproached me with his eyes, which was perhaps worse, and then with his questions. Why had I not asked his mother, if advice was needed? Why had I invited Mama in private to our home, when he had asked me not to do so?

I might have thrown myself at my husband's feet, clasping his knees, and begged him to forgive me. He might have laughed, then, and made light of it. "Do what you must," Mama would say. "Manage your man, keep on the right side of him. Be practical." But I would not be practical with Theo. I wanted to be honest.

We quarreled, and then had no chance to mend our quarrel. With the approach of the great festival, Theo was banished from our room. We did not spend any time alone together, in case some enemy tried to say I was not pure and chaste. It made a distance between us that we could not bridge.

My world was suddenly full of old men and women. Even Theo seemed to me old, his head full of tax plans and treasury reports. I interrupted him in midsentence after dinner one night. "Talk to my father about the Treasury," I told him rudely. "Permit me to spend some time with Bouly, if you please. It's still cold, but the snowdrops are in blossom; buds are forming on the wild plum trees. Newby is miserable in her pen. I know just how she feels."

"Phano!" Mother's open hand slapped against my head. "You sound like a spoiled brat."

"Mother," said Theo quietly, "Phano has a big job

ahead. She has been working hard to be ready. We forget how young she is."

Mother and son looked at each other. "You don't have to treat me like a child!" I shouted. Then my tears overflowed.

Mother patted my shoulder. "I'm sorry I lost my temper," she said quietly. "Your husband is right. Theo, I will take the girls out to the country. It's still cold, but we'll wrap ourselves in warm cloaks. No doubt Phano's goose will guard us, she's a fierce one! I'll invite a friend or two." She pondered. "Helen, maybe. Yes, it's the perfect opportunity."

I blew my nose. "Who is Helen? Do I know her?"

"You met her at Bouly's party. Tall, my age, her hair is grayer than mine, though I think her maid touched it up that day. Now, what did she wear? You'd remember; she likely wove it herself. A rose-colored tunic, I think."

"With golden threads? And a matching cloak, but darker rose. Beautiful work. You are right, somebody introduced us. I don't remember what we talked about; it was only a few words. I didn't know she was a weaver."

Mother looked at me intently. "She really wants to know you better."

"Helen can keep you company while the girls have a good romp," said Theo. "Don't forget a ball or two. Will you take Minta, and Battus from the stables, for escort?"

Not the next day, but the day after that, we drove out of Athens under a pallid sun. It was cold, but the air was like an elixir. When you live in a big city, you learn not to notice how bad it smells. I probably go around with my nose half closed most of the time. My nostrils open wide in the country, though, and I suck in everything, individual scents and glorious mixtures of grass, hay, wild onions, mint, oak trees, olive or cedar. That day, Bouly and I filled our lungs with the odor of freshly turned earth. We picked early plum blossoms and petted the black mare's silver-gray foal. Newby followed me more closely than any dog.

Mother and her friend had made a picnic. When it was time to eat, we spread rugs on the ground. Helen sat down beside me. Newby rushed at her, wings flapping, and would have bitten the poor woman if I had not moved. Bouly held the goose, who kept up her raucous squawks while I apologized. "Better you should visit me," Helen shouted. "Leave Newby home, so we can get acquainted."

Helen's cloak was woven in shades of gray, dark blending into light. If I had been sitting closer, or if Newby had been quiet, I could have asked about her weaving. "I would like to visit you," I called back, "but we'll have to wait until after the Anthesteria. I'm sorry."

"After the Anthesteria," Helen echoed. "Good." Her face was dark, as if she spent many hours outdoors. Today her hair was unashamedly gray, flecked with strands of black.

We ate pieces of chicken, goat cheese, oat bread and honey cakes, washed down with well-watered wine. I pretended I was only a girl, and not the Basilinna of Athens, soon to be married to Dionysos himself.

# seventeen

The first of Anthesterion arrived. The new moon was a sliver in the night sky, Artemis showing the least of her beauty and power. On the eleventh day of this month, the jars would be opened and the great festival named for this month would begin.

On the fourth day, I met the fourteen priestesses. *Hera aid me, Dionysos aid me,* I thought, *they are all as old and liver spotted and toothless as their leader who has taught me. What man would want any one of them?* I was less kind in my thoughts because of my separation from Theo. I missed talking to him, just the two of us, as much as I missed the warmth of his strong arms. *It will be a farce,* I thought, *to ask these dried-up prunes if they are chaste.*

I should have known better. White hair and wrinkles do not mean the end of desire, for men or women either. The day before the festival, a man was caught coming from one of the old priestesses' rooms. She was not chaste. My teacher made me join in examining her. Disgusting—the wretch had not even washed. We found a replacement quickly, however. I could see this had happened before. The substitute knew her duties perfectly.

When we were both satisfied, I sat with the high priestess. "The gods be thanked you kept good watch." I spoke from my heart. "If that woman had joined us and had sworn falsely, she would have profaned my Anthesteria—and endangered Athens."

"Yes," said the priestess. "You have courage, young Basilinna. I saw that in the beginning, although I was urged to suspect you. Trust me, I have kept good watch over *everyone*. You will keep faith with the god, even if danger comes to you because of it."

She had kept watch on me, had she? At another time, I might have been angry. Now I did not spare it a thought, except to be relieved that she took nothing for granted. Danger to me? What did she mean? A chilling thought leaped into my mind. "What will happen to that woman?" I asked.

"She will be whipped and sent home in disgrace. She will never be permitted to attend a festival again in Athens. If she dares to enter a temple, any temple, in the future, she risks the same treatment as an adulteress:

anybody who recognizes her may beat her to the point of death. Anyone can tear her earrings from her ears, the necklace from her neck, the clothes from her back, actions that would otherwise deserve strict punishment." She spoke as a judge, without passion, without human feeling of any kind.

I shivered. Why would anyone take such a risk?

"Will you keep her a prisoner until I can question her?" I asked.

The old woman paused to look at me. "You may question her," she answered slowly. "Torture her, if you wish. Without torture, she probably won't answer you." I could see she was about to tell me she wished to be present, so I spoke up.

"If I find any conspiracy, any threat of blackmail, anything you might want to know, I will send for you at once," I assured her.

"Very well." She shrugged. "Little doubt it will turn out to be mere foolishness, nothing more. Now, we must both put it out of our minds." She smiled, a smile of great sweetness, and I saw that one might love her, not only fear her or hold her in awe.

Anthesteria is the festival of the new wine. It is the earliest great festival of spring, when the first blossoms have begun to show and the wine from the fall harvest is ready to drink. Anthesteria means "flowers," and many children wear crowns of blossoms. Dionysos, god of wine, returns from the Underworld. The Basilinna marries him, and from their union the whole world is reborn.

Father, Mama and I had always celebrated Anthesteria quietly at home. We were in the minority, though. The public celebrations were open to everybody, citizens, foreign born, even slaves. This year, as usual, most people would put on their best clothes, garland their heads with wreaths, and join the crowds.

The first day was wine tasting, and the festival of the little jars. Leaders in the ceremonies were mostly men. The nine archons, Theo at their head, took turns bending over three or four of the huge jars, drawing the wine fumes into their nostrils. From their smiles, from the relaxation of their tense bodies, everybody could tell that this year's wine was good. Dionysos be praised!

Servants of the god passed out little jars of the sweet new wine, along with water for mixing. Dora came to walk beside me as the triumphant procession formed and moved off. Trumpets brayed; cymbals clashed. Everybody cheered. As the women near me saw who I was, many of them cheered for me. "The Basilinna!" "Praise Dionysos, the Basilinna!" resounded in my ears.

In the men's group across the road, Theo saw me and waved. Then somebody pushed through the group of archons. Even before I saw the squat figure and the sneering face with the bulging eyes, I knew him: Phrynion. Fat Bardian pushed through behind him. Theo nodded, smiled, clapped them on the shoulder. I knew he was only being diplomatic, but it felt as if my husband were betraying me too.

Before I saw them, I felt as tall as two houses. Now I felt myself shrink, as small as a mouse. Dora's hand gripped mine. "Steady, Phano," she said quietly. "Let the men lead off; we'll follow them. Brace yourself on my arm. If you feel faint, don't let anyone see."

The men turned into the road, the archons leading. My shoulders felt lighter when they had passed. I breathed in, deep, and sighed the air out again. Dora's arm was firm, though no one could see that she was supporting me. My legs felt like legs again, not bent reeds. People were still cheering for me; now I could hear their cheers.

"Are you ready, Mother?" I asked, as I were letting her set the pace.

"I am ready, Basilinna. Thank you, Daughter." Dora's quick, mischievous grin was as reassuring as her unusually loud voice. The road here was broad and smooth, with shallow grassy ditches on each side. The women of Athens followed us as we followed the men toward the shrine of Dionysos in the Marshes, the ancient shrine where my fourteen priestesses and I would stand tomorrow morning.

The shrine was low, vaulted in stone, mossy with age. The massive wooden door was still closed and barricaded halfway up by a pile of rocks. The altars for tomorrow's sacrifice had been set up, rough blocks of dark stone, with a shallow depression hollowed out on top. People around me shouted joyfully, but I was silent, and again the noise grew more and more distant. The sacred place seemed to make its own silence and draw me in. Dora finally pinched me. "I've been shouting at you," she said anxiously. "I would not wish to call you back from a vision, Phano, but the archons are about to make their libation. I know you want to hear it."

"Thank you, Mother."

The men poured wine from their small jars. "Hear our prayer, great Dionysos!" they cried. "May this year's wine be harmless to all. May it bring health and happiness and all good things to us, and to all who drink it." Theo was the tallest of the archons, the youngest, and the best looking; his mother and I agreed about that.

The processions broke into groups of family and friends as we walked to the meadows. That day's competitions began, all honoring Dionysos: puppets, flutes, singers to the lyre, children's choruses. As the day passed, I kept looking for signs of danger, but Phrynion and Bardian had vanished.

That night, I slept in the temple of Dionysos, halfway up the steep Acropolis, with Athene and the Parthenon at the summit keeping watch. The priestesses had made my bed in an inner room. Without my wool basket my hands were restless, but I composed my mind at last and fell asleep, and dreamed.

In the dream, I struggled to give birth, squatting over the birthing couch. The midwife had her hands open to catch the baby, but it was not a baby; it was a serpent that came from my womb. I put it to my breast, but it did not suckle. It bit my nipple; my blood flowed, bright red blood mixed with my white milk. My nipple still felt tender when I woke, but I was not in pain, and there was no blood—or milk.

What could it mean? Was I unfit to play my part in the Mysteries? I longed to ask Mama, or Dora, or even Theo, though this dream was surely for a woman to explain. What would happen if I told the old priestess, and she judged me unfit? Would she have a new wife for Theo, as well trained as I, ready to take my place? Whatever her judgment, she would act on it, no matter that she liked me and thought me brave.

What would happen if I kept silent and found out later I had committed sacrilege? The gods might punish Athens for my crime.

I could not risk it. I rose at once and asked for the old crone. Head bowed, I waited for her verdict.

"Basilinna, this is a true dream, sent by the god," she told me. "This serpent is Zeus the Kindly, who takes that form. This serpent is also the servant of Asclepius the healer. This serpent twines about the staff of Hermes, messenger of the gods, who leads the souls of the dead to the Underworld. This serpent is Athene's symbol from her shield, where she carries the head of Medusa with the snaky locks. This serpent is Athens. You nourish Athens from your body, with both blood and milk. Great is the god. This is a dream of joy. I have brought your robes for the ceremony, lady. Let us dress you for this happy marriage."

A second priestess stepped forward, her arms full of dark cloth. Two of them fastened the old-fashioned peplos at my shoulders with golden pins, so long they could have pierced a human heart. One bore the bull's head of Crete, the other, the snaky head of Gorgon Medusa, who turned all men to stone.

"I have never seen pins so long." I stretched my hand, measuring. The pin caught my thumb, and I gasped in pain. A drop of bright blood oozed, scarlet against the gold.

"Offer it to the god," commanded the priestess.

"Great Dionysos," I murmured. The priestess squeezed my thumb.

"Another good sign, like your dream." She smiled again.

In the half-light before dawn, my procession set out for the sanctuary in the marshes. We were a straggly lot. I strode ahead; my priestesses followed; other women of Athens followed them, all at our own pace. The air was crisp and cold; frost silvered the grass. When we reached the shrine, the rocks had been cleared. The door stood ajar, though all was dark inside. My own future, as well as the future of Athens, depended on what happened in that place today. I turned my back on the gaping entrance. My fourteen priestesses and I stood beside our altars to watch the sunrise. As my teacher had predicted, the gods had sent fair weather and unclouded skies.

In the city, the men's drinking contest would soon begin. Families would give little round-bellied wine jugs to their children. The day is called Choes; it gets its name from the short-necked, fat little jugs. Most of the competitions are geared to children and youth. There are dogcart races, ball games, wrestling, even a race for babies crawling on hands and knees, and prizes for all the winners.

Men who did not compete in the drinking contest would form today's procession to the marshes. Before they arrived, I led private rituals for the women. Standing behind my altar, I faced the others, so I was first to see the men approaching, though we all heard the shouting, singing and flute music; we all heard the little sounds of bleating from the fifteen lambs. Along with the lambs, the men brought silver bowls to catch the blood, and knives of black glass, each sharp enough to split a feather as it fell.

One by one the priestesses repeated the oath after me: "I sanctify myself and am pure and holy, from all things which are not purifying," and all the rest of it. I never hesitated. My voice was strong and clear.

Together, we stroked our knives across the lambs' velvet throats. At each altar, an assistant steadied the silver bowl and caught the blood. "Accept our sacrifice, Lord Dionysos," we prayed. "May our crops flourish; may all our ewes bear twin lambs; may every cow be freshened." When we had asked Dionysos to help our crops grow, we asked him also to bless the city, to make Athens flourish, to yield a harvest of righteousness and wisdom, of decent behavior and right thinking, of respect for families and for the laws.

In front of everyone, I made my vow that I was pure and holy. I made my vow to enter into sacred union with the god. The winter sun was almost at its height, warming my head and shoulders. I would not break my fast until we returned to the city, but I felt neither hunger nor thirst.

The ancient priestess put a small lamp into my right hand. I turned my back on the crowd and faced the sanctuary. Surely this shrine was old a thousand years ago, when the men of Greece sailed away to Troy. The low structure was shaped like a barrel that has been cut in half lengthwise. Over the centuries, earth had piled up around the walls, or the walls had sunk into the ground; I walked down a slope to the door.

The dark entrance yawned; I had to bend my head to pass inside. Behind me, the heavy wooden door swung shut. I shivered in the stone-vaulted room. I walked forward steadily toward a low block of stone, where I set down the lamp. Into the edge of the dim light came a figure heavily cloaked, its face hidden behind a mask of gold. I bowed my head. "Lord," I said, "I am here to be your bride."

I breathed deep, willing my heart to slow its furious beating.

He advanced slowly, his heavy footsteps echoing on the stone floor. Trembling, I sank to my knees. Who was this being? I had schooled myself to welcome the god, however he might come, but in this presence I felt threatened, not overawed. My nerves tingled. I ached to strip off the golden mask. *Stop these impious thoughts,* I told myself. *You are a priestess in a sacred place. Whatever happens here, the god intends it.*

Then the cloaked figure stood in front of me. His

hands closed on my shoulders. I raised my face and drew in a shuddering breath. In an instant of horror, I knew exactly who he was. The air was full of his stinking breath. "Phrynion! You!"

He had no warning, or he might have been able to hold me. As I named him, I jumped to my feet, throwing off his hands. With one blow, I knocked the gilded disguise from his lying face.

"You are here to be my bride," he mocked me.

"Never!"

He stepped closer. "Filth!" I spat out the insult. "You'll never get away with this."

He roared with laughter. "It's the perfect joke, my dear. I won't appear in the matter at all. Trust me, it's arranged. You'll be soiled, but not by any union with a god. The old priestess will see at once that you have profaned the Mystery. Your whole body will tell her. If she hesitates to do her duty, one of your priestesses will remind her. Do you come willingly, Phano, or must I force you?"

I aimed my knee at his crotch, a trick Mama taught me, but the beast sidestepped me and seized my arms. He threw me down on the floor and tumbled on top of me, snickering. His fat lips ground against mine.

At that moment, a great power entered into me. My thumbs felt for my enemy's eyes. He screamed, high and thin; it was a pity that I could not pause to savor the sound. Phrynion was not tall, but he was heavy and strong. I threw him off me, and threw him down as if he had been nothing more than a sack of flour. His head hit the corner of the stone table as he fell. Wonder of wonders, he lay quietly. I held the lamp to inspect: his eyes were glazed. Blood streamed from his nose. With one foot, I rolled him onto his side, but he did not stir.

The old priestess had promised that I would be guided. Raising the lamp, I looked around, but the ancient stones held no message that I could read. Perhaps there would be no bridegroom. Phrynion had profaned my festival. Clearly, Dionysos was not here. Would the god punish Athens for Phrynion's sacrilege?

At last, the air around me thickened into mist, and I heard, no, I felt a voice drawing me forward. The mist parted to reveal steps of stone, worn by many feet, descending into darkness. "Come," the voice beckoned. "Put down the lamp; you have no need of it."

My rage had passed, leaving me cleansed in spirit. Descending, I could not see the steps, yet the way was clear and my feet sure. In a chamber below, the true god waited for his bride. I am forbidden to describe our union. Enough that my sacred marriage would bring no shame ever, no discomfort between my dear husband and myself. Union it was, for all that, and the power of the god for the good of Athens entered into me. Humbly I received that power, knowing it was not for me or mine but only for the city, dearer to me than my own life.

After a time, how long I could not say, the god left that place and I found the stairs. In the room above, the mists had disappeared. On the floor, Phrynion gave a snort. He lay curled like a baby on his side.

What should I do with that evil man? A short time ago, it had been easy to pick him up and throw him down again. However, that incredible strength had passed. I might still drag him outside. Wine—and my cry of sacrilege—would madden the crowd. I savored a vision of Phrynion being torn to pieces.

As I bent over him, however, cold logic spoke. People who saw and heard me now would be convinced that I spoke the truth. Not many people, however, would actually see and hear me. How long before rumor changed the story to make me a partner in Phrynion's sacrilege? If the rain was late, or early; if the crops failed; if a calf died, or a child, they would curse my name as well as his. For now, Phrynion was better left inside the shrine.

Smiling, I opened the door. The aura of the god enveloped me. I felt as tall as a mountain. The old priestess knelt, tears streaming down her face. The whole crowd followed her lead. "Behold the bride of the god! Behold the savior of Athens!" They sounded like the sea. Borne on waves of sound, Theo came forward. He too knelt at my feet.

I was quick to raise them both. The crowd cheered even louder as we stood before them.

"Savior of Athens," said my husband, "you have triumphed, and all Athens knows it. I am very proud that you are my wife. I am also glad that you are not called on to do this every day."

"Once is enough," said the old priestess. "This will be a prosperous year for Athens. I have never witnessed such power."

The young men pulled the sacred cart toward the three of us, the cart all gold and ivory, and the youths in white tunics, each head wreathed with gold. The priestess crowned me too with a wreath of golden leaves, myrtle, olive and oak, three times as rich as the others.

They lifted us into the cart. I raised my arms, and the crowd fell silent. No bird sang; no baby cried; such was the power within me. My voice rang in triumph. "People of Athens, hear the god's voice. Your enterprises will prosper. Your harvests will be bountiful. Your sheep will bear twin lambs. No enemy will rise against Athens in the coming year. Thus it shall be. Now let the door be closed. Bring rocks, and seal up the shrine."

As I watched, the door swung shut. Pairs of slaves began to roll huge rocks against it. Others strained to add smaller stones to the growing pile. I would have watched until they finished, but Theo pulled at my hand. "Turn around, Basilinna," he said. "Your work here is done."

I turned my back on Phrynion with mixed feelings. If the gods willed it, he would die in the shrine he had profaned. Athens would be better off without him, and I would be safer. I am not a bloodthirsty person, but I really did not care if Phrynion starved. Likely he would not die, however. He had not entered the shrine without help. The people who had opened the sacred place once would open it again.

While I had watched the shrine, another procession had formed, this one led by girls with cymbals and flutes. Young men in white tunics seized the long reins; our cart lurched forward. Singing and rejoicing, the people of

Athens brought me and my husband, along with the priestess, to the feast. I stood, so that more people could see and feel the power of the god. Other people gathered their cloaks closer as the shadows lengthened, but I loosened mine. I needed no cloak to keep me warm.

The day passed into evening while we ate and drank; with the hours, slowly, the god's power passed from me. At last, my great work was officially complete. The ancient priestess kissed me on both cheeks. My husband waited with his chariot. I still felt some remnant of power when I mounted, but I leaned back against Theo more and more as he drove, and welcomed his strong arms when he lifted me down at last inside our own courtyard.

# eighteen

When Dionysos comes up from the Underworld on the second day of the festival, he leaves the entrance open. Even a crack is enough. On the third and last day of Anthesteria, the spirits of the dead swarm up to the land of the living and roam about until nightfall. Then we yell, "Get out, goblins, the Anthesteria is over!" They have to go back. If we can protect ourselves and our homes throughout the day, we are safe for another year.

Theo got up before dawn to smear our door with pitch. Ghosts stay away from pitch; they don't want to get stuck in it. We gave buckthorn for chewing to everybody in the house. "Keep some in your mouth all day," I reminded them. "Don't forget to take extra if you have to go out."

The day was warm, though no doubt there would be more cold days before spring really arrived. I wished Theo and I could have stayed quietly at home, but we both had work to do. Theo had to make a sacrifice of wheat flour and honey for the ghosts at the chasm near the Olympieion.

I would finally be able to question the impure priestess who had tried to profane my ritual. She was confined in the temple of Dionysos. Outside the temple, people performed rituals to appease angry ghosts and send them back to the Underworld. Inside, I discovered that the wicked priestess would soon be joining them. She had drunk a cup of hemlock, the executioner's poison.

She was still living when I reached her, though her eyes were cloudy. I seized her hands, to pull her up, but dropped them with a shudder. They were cold as winter ice. She knew me, though. With a great effort, she raised herself on an elbow. "Your enemy is powerful," she gasped; then she fell back. That was all.

I gave certain orders at the temple, then hurried to the chasm. Theo might still be there. If he had completed his offering, I was ready to make my own.

The ghost of the dead priestess would pass below me on her way to the Styx, the black river which all spirits must cross on their way to Tartarus. She had no money to pay the ferryman. I had forbidden them at the temple to put coins in her mouth. Theo had left. Just as well; I would not have to waste time on explanations. I poured out my wheat and honey and held up two copper obols.

"Hear me, new ghost, you who were a priestess of Dionysos," I intoned. "I will pay your passage. Without me, you will wander forever, wailing on the riverbank. I charge you, tell me the name of my enemy."

"You know his name." Did I hear those words, or did I imagine them, whispered out of the depths? I knew my enemy: Phrynion.

❀

I walked home slowly. Minta walked behind me, as she had done all day, a welcome change from my constant companions of the past months, free women who could swear, if called on, that I had kept myself pure.

At last, I could pick up the threads of my life. At the feast the day before, Bouly had bent over and put her mouth to my ear. "I must see you," she had whispered. "Can you stay home tomorrow afternoon?"

At the time, I had been beyond cogent thought. Now I was rested, and there was time to worry. What could be so urgent? Had Bouly's face been radiant or terrified? What was the matter with me, that I truly did not know? If only we could be girls again together, Little Bears of Artemis!

Newby had been banished from the house while I was busy with priestesses. Poor Newby could not understand that she did not need to protect me from them. Or else she understood better than I did. Whichever, it was time, and more than time, she came back to her proper place. Bouly would want to see her as well. I beckoned to Minta.

"Minta, bring Newby inside as soon as we're home. Set out my workbasket and my yarn."

"Things are getting back to normal, are they?" said Minta. "That's good news, Mistress, but Newby is sitting on a clutch of eggs. We had to do something to keep her from chasing after you. We knew you had no time for her, but Newby didn't know. You don't want me to take her off her nest, I hope. Wait until the goslings hatch."

"I've been so busy, I didn't even ask. Poor Newby. Will she still want me, when she has babies of her own?"

"Certainly. I know about geese."

"That's good." I wasn't sure that *I* knew about anything for certain anymore. Except spinning: I knew about that. It was a comforting thought.

I shivered. Suddenly I felt sure Bouly would bring ghastly news. Mama sometimes has these sudden feelings, but I don't. Besides, Mama is not always right. There was no reason for this horrid fear. Try as I would, however, I could not shake it. The smell of death stuck in my nostrils. My hands still felt the dying priestess's icy grasp. What bad news did Bouly have for me?

In my wildest moments, I could not have guessed how bad her news would be. Bouly was shy with other people, but she had never been lost for words with me. That day, even her hug of greeting was awkward. Her eyes met mine and skittered away again. She swallowed, asked for water, swallowed again. It was a long time since I had noticed how big Bouly was, how ungainly; now it was hard to see anything else.

"Out with it, Bouly," I said at last.

That brought her tears, great shaking sobs. It was an improvement; at least our hug now felt the way it should.

"Oh, Phano," she sobbed; then she broke down totally again. It seemed forever until she pulled herself together enough to say what needed to be said. I wish I had never needed to hear it.

In the years before she knew me, Bouly would shut her ears and turn her thoughts elsewhere at the first hint of politics. After we became friends, she listened to the talk around her.

Nobody noticed the change. We had laughed about it. Athenian men must think their wives and daughters are like their favorite couches, comfortable and brainless. Except for Theo. Father. Uncle Nikos. Maybe a few more, although I have not met them.

"I wanted to tell you, I'm going to be married," Bouly sobbed at last.

"That's wonderful! Hera help us, Bouly, why are you crying? Is he old and ugly, then? A widower with ten children? Surely your father loves you better than that!"

Bouly gave a hiccuppy giggle, followed by more sobs. "He's a friend of Theo's," she sobbed. "Last night, I thought we'd be like sisters, and now everything is wrecked and I can't ever see you again."

"Can't see me again? Bouly, did I hear you right? What's going on?"

"No, I can't," she hiccupped. "Never, never. You're a slave, but that's not the worst of it. You've brought a curse on Athens." She clung to me. It was difficult to loosen her arms enough to catch my breath.

*The goblins are in my house; I'll never be rid of them.* I felt nothing but dull wretchedness.

Then I straightened my shoulders. Mama has not brought me up to fall into despair. "You are wrong, Bouly. Whoever told you that is wrong. These are more of Phrynion's lies."

"Bardian is convinced," she said dully. "Whatever proof he showed, my father believed it. He did not want to believe it, but he did. Father is not a fool. I'm not allowed to see you."

"Do you believe I would bring a curse on Athens?"

"Knowingly? Never!" Her eyes flashed; then she slumped again.

"You believe this," I said slowly. "You don't believe I knew it, but you do believe I committed sacrilege."

"I'm sure of it." Bouly sounded as weary as I had felt. Was it only the day before?

I felt a thousand years old at that moment, and heavy as earth. This was where my dreams had led. My wool basket lay beside me, the old thigh shield on top of the fleeces waiting to be spun. Sudden rage flooded through me. I seized the pottery piece in both hands, raised it high above my head, and threw it crashing down on the hearthstones. Shattered bits flew everywhere. Bouly stared, aghast.

"Phano, what have you done?"

I bent and picked up a fragment by my foot. The head

of one of the little partridges looked back at me, with one black eye. "I think I will kill Phrynion." My voice was calm. "I wish I had Mama's old brooch, Hippolyta with her spear, but Mama is not to know until I have killed him. Minta has a black knife, very sharp, she'll give it to me."

"Such talk! You, who could hardly bear to kill a lamb in sacrifice? Have the Furies possessed you?"

"Killing Phrynion may not save Athens, but it will put a spoke through Philip's chariot wheel. Without Phrynion, the rich men's party will fall apart, for a while at least. Theo needs all the time he can get."

"This is wild talk, Phano. Theo won't thank you for it. If you murder Phrynion, your husband will be destroyed. Who will believe he had no share in it?"

My arms fell. Bouly was right. "I've never seen you like this," she went on. "I'm sending for Theo. He needs to know what's happening. Where's Minta?"

"Visiting Newby on her nest. I gave her leave."

"Fine. I'll go myself."

I stared at the mess on the floor until they came back together. Theo bent and picked up the little partridge head. "Your thigh shield!" He sounded shocked. "You didn't tell me about this, Bouly. No wonder Phano is upset."

I laughed. It seemed better than screaming, as I might have done. "Tell us the whole story, Bouly; don't leave anything out."

"Bardian came to our house this morning. He brought

167

Nerissa." *Pig-Woman*. "They did not speak to me," Bouly continued, "but Bardian began talking before Father had shut the door. I heard one sentence: 'Theo will have to divorce her now.' Hera help me, Phano, this was about *you*.

"There's no place where I could spy on the men. If Mother took Nerissa upstairs, though, I had a chance. I ran up and sat down behind the loom. A minute later, I heard them on the stairs. They never looked for me. They didn't think of me at all.

"Nerissa was in full flood," Bouly continued bitterly. "She said, 'Phano is a slave. She is Nera's daughter. Nera was a slave. That arbitration, Phrynion only agreed to it because of our family. He did not want to offend my husband by making a fool of Theo. Theo is an important member of our family. Better a fool than a ruined man, I'd say.'

"She was positively gloating! I don't know how I kept still; my tongue hurts where I bit it. Mother said something then, 'That's terrible,' I think. She sounded shocked.

"'Terrible! It's worse than terrible,' Nerissa raved on. 'Phano has married into our family. It's a disgrace. Both her parents were Phrynion's slaves. The child was born in his home. Nera didn't run away from Phrynion. She wronged him, and he sold her, but we both know that the slave child belongs to the master. Phano belongs to Phrynion. He has proved it. He has also proved that Stephanos's daughter died when she was a baby. Nera has no shame and no scruples. Such airs she puts on! We'll rub her nose in the mud where she belongs.'

"Mother asked, rather faintly, what they planned to do. 'Phrynion will sue Stephanos for passing off that courtesan as his citizen wife, and for marrying her daughter to an archon, the King Archon. It's an insult to all the proper wives and daughters of Athens.'

" 'Phano is Bouly's friend,' said Mother. 'I can't believe this, Nerissa. It's hard to believe even Nera would do anything so wicked. Phano is very young, but from all I've seen and heard, she has high principles. Until anything changes, she is our relation by marriage. Bardian does not yet speak for our family. What does Uncle Nikos say?' "

"I've always admired your mother," said Theo softly.

"She was about to get even more of a shock." Bouly sighed. "Have you heard about Uncle Nikos?"

"What about him?"

"He can't say anything." Tears dripped down Bouly's cheeks. "If the gods have not cursed Athens, they have surely cursed our family."

"Tell us, Bouly. Leave curses out of it for now. Uncle Nikos cannot say anything. Why not?"

"They took him home last night after the feast. Bardian followed his father to the room where he sleeps. Nerissa said they had to discuss some family concerns. We can guess what they were! All of a sudden there was a crash. Bardian yelled for help. He said Uncle Nikos turned blue and fell on the floor. He is alive. His eyes move, but he cannot speak. He lies at Bardian's home now, and the doctors say he may never recover. Bardian speaks as head of this family." Bouly drew a ragged breath.

169

She looked at me, then at Theo. "I think I can remember every word that nasty woman said. If Nerissa can go on being a member of our family, and Phano cannot, there is no justice among men or gods."

"Bardian speaks as head of our family," Theo mused. "I have feared this day. Even a flimsy story may be accepted when it is so very convenient for so many powerful people."

I shuddered. Theo's lips tightened to a thin line. "This is very bad news, Bouly, but we have not heard it all. Go on. Bardian speaks for the family. What did dear Cousin Nerissa say next?"

"She said, 'Theo will have to resign. My husband told him it was a mistake to give a key job to Stephanos. Slime sticks, my dear. Some of Stephanos's slime will stick to Theo. Bardian says we can all sleep easier: with Stephanos and Theo gone, the high tax party in Athens is dead.'"

"I knew it." Theo was bitter. "That's what this is about. The fools will hand over Athens to Philip of Macedon without a fight. Goddess Athene, how can we save your city now?"

"I don't believe this accusation is true," I said. "About me, I mean, about who I am."

"Nor do I," said Theo at once.

"Then you can put it right," said Bouly eagerly.

"I don't think so." "I doubt it." Theo and I spoke at the same time. Theo went on. "We like to believe the worst of each other here in Athens. This story will spread all over the city; it will get worse with every telling. Years ago, Stephanos had that problem with his friend. There was no

170

proof Stephanos ever knew the money had been stolen. I do not for a moment believe he knew it, if only because Stephanos is much too canny to be part of something so stupid. That old story will be raked up again, though; it will be held against him."

"Nobody can accuse you of anything like that," I said.

"I gave your father a job," said Theo. "I married his daughter, my darling. The most powerful men in Athens will have to spend a great deal of money if my tax policies come into effect. A few of them see the need, but most do not. They never wanted me as archon." He tugged at his golden beard.

He went on, "If I resign at once, Stephanos too, no help for it, maybe they won't go after us in court. Phrynion wouldn't dare to sue Stephanos in person after the settlement I arranged; it would cost him too much if he were to lose. Someone else would have to bring the suit, even though he would be behind it.

"Bardian does not like me, but I think he would be relieved if the family name is not disgraced in court, and the family fortune, or my part of it, is not spent in defending Stephanos, and through him, me. I'll offer to resign. Maybe we can retire to the farm, Phano; you'd like it there. I'll resign on one condition: Phrynion must drop this suit. He must give me his promise in writing, before witnesses, not to renew it. On my part, I'll commit to play no further part in politics. If Phrynion has any kind of evidence, no doubt he'll take good care to keep it. That way, he can be sure I won't break my part of the agreement."

"Theo, you can't!"

"I can, dear wife. I can't do anything else, more's the pity. Nor can your father and mama," he added. "They will have to leave Athens. I can't help them, not just now. Let us hope Stephanos has saved his money. He and Nera can live pleasantly enough in some small town—in the west, perhaps, or on one of the islands. If I still have friends after the dust settles, there may be a chance of a minor government job. We'll both have to get out of politics."

"Are you trying to talk me into this, or to persuade yourself?" I asked at last. My voice sounded hoarse. "I have another plan. Bouly, dear, you should go now. Thank you. And Bouly, whatever your father says, we will still be friends."

"I thought you would hate me," said Bouly.

"You get married, Bouly, and be happy," I ground out, "even if I can't dance at your wedding."

We couldn't see well through our tears, but we stumbled together and held each other, all three of us. "You've brought bad news," said Theo, "but you've given us warning. Every hour is precious now. This is war, Bouly. I'm glad you are on our side."

Theo and I heard Bouly's heavy feet on the stairs, and the distant clang of the outer door.

"Go away, goblins, the Anthesteria is over." Theo's voice resonated with an ironic echo in my mind. "Can we send them back to the Underworld, where they belong?"

"I have a plan," I told him. "If your mother will help us, something may be saved. We cannot abandon Athens without a fight."

"Tell me your plan," he replied. "If it's what I guess, I won't agree."

"Don't guess, then," I snapped.

"You sound exactly like your mama!"

"Just as well if I do." I tried to smile at him. "If ever there was a time to be practical, this is it."

Minta ran into the room before I could summon her. "Mistress, Mistress," she sobbed. Then she stubbed her toe on broken pottery. Her eyes went to the floor. "Your thigh shield. It can't be!"

"It's only pottery," I said.

"Only pottery," Minta echoed. "Is there a curse on this house?"

"Get a grip on yourself," I told her. Minta is a slave. I have responsibilities. "This is urgent. Find Mother. Tell her, from me, Theo and I must see her without delay. We'll come to her."

"I must go and look for Newby," said Minta. "I beg of you, let me go."

"Isn't Newby on her nest?" I said stupidly. "Don't tell me something has happened to her on top of everything else."

"She's gone, and the gate is open."

*Did you leave it open?* My face must have betrayed my thought.

"I didn't do it, I swear I didn't," Minta wailed. "Her eggs will hatch, and she won't be there."

I slapped her face. "Stop bawling, Minta, and tell me what has happened."

She stopped at once and stared at me. Her face was white, except for the cheek I had slapped, which quickly turned bright red.

"Don't look at me like that," I told her. "Whatever it is, I won't sell you to the mines at Laurion. Indeed, if Phrynion has his way, I might be sent there myself. Now, out with it."

My words terrified her even more. Her eyes went to the floor, to me, to the floor.

"Tell us, Minta," said Theo, very gently.

"Newby," she gulped. "I shut the gate and latched it, I know I did, but Newby is gone. She isn't anywhere. I checked the stables and the hen house. I took the broody hen off her nest and put her on Newby's eggs to keep them warm. Let me look for her."

"You stupid woman." My thigh shield lay in pieces, my friend was never to speak to me again, my relatives believed I was slave born, my husband would have to divorce me—and my goose was gone. If I'd had a whip, or even a stick, I'd have used it on her back. "This is *your* carelessness, Minta. Who else goes near Newby's pen?" Newby was always fierce, but she would be fiercer now, with a nest to protect. She always welcomed me, and tolerated Minta and Theo, but no one else. "Go and find my goose," I ordered her, "and don't come back until you do."

"I'll go to my mother," said Theo as the door swung shut behind Minta. He led me to my little armless chair. My wool basket and spindle were beside it, but not, of course, my thigh shield. Bits of it crunched under my feet.

"Sit down," said my husband gently. "I'll have a word with Mother and be back for you. Sit here and calm yourself."

Dear Theo. How could I bear to live without him? I thought I'd never be able to stop crying, but by the time he came back, I had combed my hair and was sitting quietly. I was still the Basilinna, though probably not for long.

"You may be present," I told Theo, "on condition you say nothing, not one word, until your mother and I have finished our discussion."

"Indeed? I am pleased that you permit so much."

"It's not a time for sarcasm," I told him. "You may stay because it's practical. You will understand better if you hear us, and I won't have to explain twice over." Theo sighed. He shrugged and led the way.

# nineteen

A day before, it would have been impossible for me to tell Dora what had happened. Now that nothing mattered, it was easy enough. I might have been telling a story about someone else. "I deceived you, my family deceived you," I ended drearily. "That's Phrynion's story. You can be sure he'll make the most of it. Apparently Bardian believes it. Perhaps Uncle Nikos believes it as well. If so, my actions have had a part in his illness, perhaps in his death.

"I had no right to hear the sacred rituals, let alone to lead the priestesses and become the bride of the god. How should Athens not be punished for my sacrilege?

"For my part, Mother, if this is true, it was done in ig-

norance. You may think less hardly of me, knowing that—
if you believe me."

Theo had kept quiet as I talked. He knew I would send
him away if he did not; there was no arguing with me that
day. His hand on my arm tightened from time to time. I
knew there would be bruises on my skin. "I can't divorce
you," he burst out. "Surely the gods cannot wish it. You
did nothing knowingly. There must be another way."

His mother and I both stared at him. "Get a grip on
yourself, Theo," said Dora briskly.

"You think ignorance is an excuse?" I said. "Remember Oedipus, Theo, who married his own mother
without knowing her. Remember Oedipus, and then tell
me that ignorance takes the curse off an evil action, or
that sacrilege done in ignorance is no sacrilege at all.
Please don't open your mouth again."

He hung his head.

"Theo must divorce me, Mother," I said. The dreadful
words were out, and I had spoken them. I plunged on
without a pause. "He must send me away publicly, and
dismiss Father in front of the Council. We ask your help in
two matters: to bring down Phrynion, and to get me safely
out of Athens."

"Are you finished?" I had expected Mother to be
shocked, but she was no more excited than if we had been
talking about a new way of cooking chicken or dyeing
yarn.

"Yes." I was finished. If there had been more to say, I
could not have said it then.

"My turn then. You are both jumping to conclusions on very slim evidence, it seems to me. Phrynion is a liar and a rabble-rouser, and your enemy. You know without asking that he is at the back of this. Why do you take this accusation seriously?"

"He has convinced Bardian and Bouly's father," I replied, sounding as wretched as I felt. "It might be easy with Bardian, but Bouly's father would demand good evidence. If they believe him, other people will as well."

"Even if we can eventually disprove it," said Theo, breaking his word again, "I will have to resign right away, Stephanos as well. We won't be able to continue our work. The cloud of suspicion will make it impossible. Surely you can see the problem."

"Something may be salvaged if Theo can separate himself from Father and me," I said. I coughed to clear my throat. "For me, divorce is the only way. I cannot even face my accuser in the courts."

"This rumor has not yet spread far," said Mother. "It may be squelched. Phano, your word is as good as Phrynion's. You cannot accuse him in public, that's true; but Theo can call the archons to meet here privately, where you *can* be heard. Your evidence will put Phrynion under strong suspicion, like a trickle of water when a lake is ready to burst through a dam. More evidence will surely follow yours. A man like Phrynion does not confine himself to attacking one person or one family. The dam will crumble. What you begin, others will finish."

"Excellent," I replied, sarcasm sharpening my voice.

"The Archons of Athens will listen to a courtesan's daughter who has profaned the mysteries. Wonders will never cease!"

"Stop that," said Mother, just as sharply. "Did you think you'd married into a family of simpletons? Did you imagine I would allow my only son to marry—with the family blessing—a woman who could not bear him citizen sons and daughters? You must think me very naïve."

She looked at me in disgust. "You thought I had nothing to teach you on your wedding night, Phano. Perhaps you were right, perhaps you were wrong. The men of Athens are convinced that they rule the world. Let them think so, since it makes them happy."

"Mother." Theo spoke slowly. He looked even more wretched than when we had begun our talk. "It is possible that Phano is Nera's daughter, much as I hate to think so. It is possible that Stephanos's daughter died. Nera is a fine woman, but if Phano is her daughter, my wife has profaned the mysteries.

"Surely your suggestion was not serious. If I call my fellow archons to listen to Phano, it's obvious we're treating this seriously. When I studied logic, I learned it's impossible to prove a negative."

"I never studied philosophy," said Dora. "Just as well, if it makes you give up."

"I'm not giving up," Theo roared. "I'm saying we cannot prove that Phano is *not* Nera's daughter. That's the fact; it means we're both done for here and now. Later, we'll mend matters as best we can. Now, it seems I must divorce my wife, and she must leave Athens as fast as possible. With all my heart I wish it were otherwise."

Dora faced me, ignoring her son. "You began this conversation by asking for my help," she said. "You wanted to defeat Phrynion and to leave Athens, in that order."

"Help me to leave quickly," I said. "If Father and I are out of the picture, surely Theo will not have to resign. Athens needs him. While you're working miracles, Mother, think up some foolproof way to discredit Phrynion."

"Help me to find a home for my wife," Theo added. "It maddens me to think of losing her." His lips quivered.

"I'm thankful you didn't try to manage this completely by yourselves," said Dora. "You would have made a pretty hash of it. Sit down, both of you. Give me a little time to think." She stared at her son, and then at me.

"You are wrong, Phano," she said at last. "And you are wrong as well, my son. You are not accustomed to taking orders from your mother, Theo, but this time, King Archon or not, I must insist." She looked at Theo anxiously, but he simply stared at her as if he did not know what to say.

"Mother," I broke in, "I respect your wisdom. Surely my husband does so as well. If you have a plan, please let us hear it."

"Theo?"

"Speak, Mother," said Theo. "Women in my life have surprised me before now, as my young wife knows. Don't hold back."

"Well then," said Dora. "This is how I see it. Phrynion is blackmailing you to force you to resign. His method is to spread lies about Phano. You are halfway to believing those lies yourselves. You say it does not matter if he is telling the truth or not. He is convincing, and you can't prove what he says is not true. Then surely he must be stopped."

"You have a way of stopping him?"

"Perhaps I have. Phano, bring Minta here, if you please."

"Tonight, nothing is as it should be," I told her. "Minta is out searching for Newby. Her pen was left open, and she's gone."

"That's a pity," Dora replied. "Theo, fetch Battus from the stables—unless he went with Minta. If he's out, fetch any of the household slaves—a man, Theo; this is no hour for a woman to be out in the streets by herself."

Dora was right. I thought of Minta, whom I had told not to come back without Newby. We had both been upset, but I should not have sent her out with no protection. She would not have asked anyone to go with her. She was wild to get on with her search. Also, I had shamed her. She would not want anyone else to know. A shiver prickled my neck.

As I expected, though not as I hoped, Theo came back with Battus, rubbing sleep from his eyes.

"Battus, you have taken plenty of messages to my friend Helen, widow of Evenus," Dora began. "Can you be sure of finding your way in the dark?"

"Yes, Mistress."

"Good. Go there now. Tell the gateman you have orders to speak to his mistress, though I'm sorry to awaken her. Ask her to come here with you. You will wait for her, but be very clear: I ask her to come at once. I'd be obliged if my friend does not keep us waiting while her maid arranges her hair."

"If this is needed, shouldn't I go?" Theo sounded confused.

"No," said his mother shortly. "Battus, what are you to say?"

"To the gateman—'Waken your mistress.' To the lady—'Come with me now, don't wait.'" Battus ticked off the two messages on his fingers.

"'Come with me now, don't wait, *please.*' All right, Battus, on your way."

"At once, Mistress."

As the door swung shut, Dora turned to me. "There is another reason why it's a bad plan for you to rush into exile in disgrace, isn't there, Daughter? Does your husband know?"

"Know *what*?" Theo was plainly exasperated. "Mother, everything is falling apart around me. You send a slave to fetch an old woman who doesn't even belong to our family, and then you make senseless conversation with my wife. *What* don't I know?"

"Ask Phano."

"Stop this bickering, I beg you." I wiped sudden tears from my eyes. "I may be pregnant, Mother; it's far too soon to know."

"There is a look in a woman's eyes," said Dora. "I can tell, within a few days. I am never wrong. You won't be enjoying breakfast for a while, if you're like most of us, though my grandchild will not be born for many months."

"If Mother Hera wills it," I replied.

"If Hera wills it," she echoed tenderly.

"Phano!" My husband looked as if someone had knocked him on the head with a club. "You're going to have a baby. My child. The gods cannot be so cruel as to separate us now."

"It changes nothing," I told him. "Do you think Phrynion won't lay claim to my child, if I am to have a child and he finds out? I must leave Athens and go into hiding, as far away as possible."

"I'll kill him." My husband's whole body swelled; his fists clenched.

"I'm sure you won't do anything so foolish," Dora said, "though the world would be cleaner without that nasty little man. Wait here, both of you, while I prepare for our guest. There is nothing more to be done until Helen arrives. I do have a reason for inviting her."

Theo and I held each other silently. As always, I felt comfortable and safe in his arms, though I knew that danger encircled both of us and the circle was tightening.

Soon Dora came back. Three slaves followed her, bringing food, drink and a table to set them on. "When did you eat last?" she asked.

"This morning, I suppose," said Theo. "How can anybody eat at a time like this?"

"Phano can," said Dora. She led me to the couch

herself and put a date into my hand. I nibbled, then took a big bite.

"I'm starving," I said. "Come on, Husband, I'm not the only one who must keep up my strength."

Once he began, Theo found himself as hungry as I, and Dora had to send for more food. The two platters, once again piled high, arrived at the same time as Helen, along with two of her servants and Battus. They all crowded into the room.

"Go down to the kitchen, all of you," Dora told the servants. "The lentil stew is hot. Help yourselves, you've done a good night's work." She looked at me. "I wish Minta were here."

"Minta?" Battus had almost reached the door.

"She went out looking for Newby," I told him.

Battus looked anxiously at me, and then at his mistress. "You want to look for her, don't you?" said Dora. "It's a good idea. When did she leave, Phano, just before Theo came to me? What was her plan? Which way did she go first?"

I confirmed the time but had to admit there was no plan, nor did I know which way Minta went. "Go first to Stephanos's home," said Dora. "If she escaped on her own, Newby may have gone there. Stop at the guardhouses as you go; ask if anybody saw Minta or the goose. If you've learned nothing on the way, ask Stephanos if he can spare a man to help you. Find out what you can, but you are to be back here well before sunup. I don't like this. Too many strange things are happening. All right, Battus, on your way." Battus moved as if there were a fire behind him.

Helen had studied me while Dora gave Battus his orders. Now she turned as Dora spoke to her. Dora was still very much in charge, but her voice softened. "Helen, my dear, thank you for coming in the middle of the night. I hope your family won't make trouble about it."

"Nothing I can't manage, Dora. It must be urgent, or you would have waited until morning."

"It is extremely urgent." Mother quickly sketched our situation. "Phrynion must be silenced," she concluded. "This is the time, Helen. They need to know."

None of this made sense to me. I had seen Helen twice: once at Bouly's party, and again at the picnic, when Newby had raised such a ruckus we couldn't hear ourselves. I had promised to visit Helen, to talk of weaving, but of course that visit had not happened. Now, as far as I could see, it never would.

"Make room, please, Theo," Helen said. "Let me sit beside your wife." She sank down beside me. She took both my hands and turned me so that we faced each other.

"Look at our hands," she said. Hers were slim, strong, with knobby knuckles and small fingernails. Except for some wrinkles and a few brown age spots, her hands were twins of mine.

Tears overflowed and ran down Helen's cheeks. She let the fold of her cloak fall to her shoulders. Her hair was loose, still lustrous and wavy. It was gray at the temples, grayer than Dora's, but dark strands mingled with silver at the back. "My hair was just like yours when I was your age," she said. "I might be shorter than you are now, old women shrink, but not by much." She drew her cloak aside. "Show me your ankles." I pulled up my tunic. Theo's grandmother, older than time, had looked at my ankles the first and only time I talked to her.

"We are family," I said slowly, remembering.

"Dearest Phano, your mother was my child." Helen covered her face with her cloak; her shoulders shook with sobs.

As soon as she put our hands together, I knew we must be related; perhaps she was a cousin, or an aunt. Helen was my grandmother! I drew back. My hands longed for my spindle, though it would not have calmed me much. I jumped up and ran to Theo. All the food I had just eaten churned in my belly. I glared at Dora.

"Forgive me, Phano," said Dora. "Try to forgive your grandmother. We both know it won't be easy. I do wish Minta were here."

"What is Minta's part in this?" Theo asked.

Helen drew back her cloak and raised her head. "Minta was my slave," she said. "She had been nursemaid to my daughter. I trusted her. I knew she would protect my grandchild with her life."

"Minta was Mama's slave," I said, "until she came here with me."

"You were always her real job," Helen said, "keeping you from harm. The secret has been a burden to her all

186

these years. She passed on information when she could." She shuddered. "Imagine my feelings when I heard about Phrynion! Certainly, Minta left out a lot of the details.

"I am repeating her words; I'm not likely to forget them. 'Phrynion and everybody in his house had to think Phano didn't matter to me. I watched more than once when he beat her. If Phrynion even suspected that I was ready to kill him, he'd have had me sent away or murdered. My hand itched to plunge my knife into his heart.'" Tears streamed down Helen's face.

"Poor Minta," I said. "If she had killed Phrynion, she would have been executed, and she would have been tortured first."

"If she had tried and failed, you would have been left without protection. I'm sure Nera did her best, but she was locked up most of the time, as I've heard."

"I thought Minta cared more about herself than me. I forgot how loyal she has been, all my life. I've been thoughtless today as well. I'm ashamed."

"Why didn't you tell us?" Theo asked. "If you couldn't tell Phano, why didn't you tell *me*? Mother? Helen?"

"It was not my secret," said his mother, "though of course I was thrilled when you wanted to marry."

"So was I," Helen added. I glared at her.

"Grandmother, why didn't my family acknowledge me?" I demanded. "There must have been some disgrace in my birth."

"No disgrace." Helen stood up and took a step toward me. Without thinking, I drew back. She stiffened. "It was an argument over money, that's all. Your grandfather died soon after your mother married Stephanos. Your great-uncles—my brothers—found one excuse after another not to hand over your mother's dowry. I begged them to honor our word, but they refused point-blank.

" 'Better to throw that dowry into the sea than give it to Stephanos,' they said. 'The Sea God's favor is worth something. Stephanos is so far in debt, his creditors will seize every obol, no matter if it really belongs to his wife. If he gets his hands on this money now, it will be lost.'

"Your great-uncles could not acknowledge you without paying the dowry. If your mother had lived, I would have shamed them into it, but she died. I did what I could."

I took a deep breath. What would Mama have said now? Dear Mama, she would be practical, of course. "I have been brought up to be practical," I said, not quite steadily. "I must thank you, Grandmother, for doing what you could."

I would never have expected Helen's arms to be so strong. She squeezed the breath from my body with her hug. I was still angry at my family's insult to me, but my rage gradually grew less. When I got my arms free, I hugged her back.

"Not too tight, Helen," said Dora. "If I'm right, you will be holding your first great-grandchild before midwinter. Phano, Nera has taught you well, I admit it freely. We are in her debt. I won't forget, nor will your grandmother, you may be sure of it." She turned to Helen. "Now, dear friend, you can see why we needed you *now*, tonight."

"A great-grandchild! Phano, that's the best possible news. Yes indeed." Helen's hand moved toward my belly. Again, I moved away. Helen shrugged. "Past is past," she said. "Now we must look to the future. A great-grandchild, Hera be praised. Our family must acknowledge Phano in public at once."

"That is why I sent for you," Dora agreed.

"Dora, I'm ahead of you. Dear Phano's Anthesteria gave me the perfect opening. All I had to do was mention Phano's name; my brothers were eager to welcome her publicly. That goes without saying: any family would be proud to include the Savior of Athens. Everybody is thrilled; the wives started planning the celebration before the goblins went back to the Underworld.

"If you had not sent for me, I would have come here in a day or two. The idea was to hold a gathering of the whole clan for the official ceremony. I know that's not usual, especially for a girl. Perhaps my brothers feel guilty for their neglect. Well, so they should. Now we'll have to move faster, but that's all right. We'll have the big gathering when the baby is born. Phano's official welcome will take place quietly tomorrow morning. Then the announcement must be made in the Agora. It can all be done before dinner."

"Will your brothers agree to move so fast?" Theo asked. "Phrynion has not given up; indeed, he talks of new charges. We've had trouble already with the leaders in our family. Won't your brothers want to delay?"

"Put me beside Nera," said Helen; "then let Phano stand between us. Who does she look like? Who is she related to? It's obvious; no one can fail to see it. My brothers aren't fools. If Phrynion says that Nera is this girl's mother, he lies, no matter what so-called proof he may wave around. That slimy toad! The more I think about it, the angrier I get. It's not only the threat to Phano; it's her husband, it's the elected government of Athens as well. My brothers will be furious; so will my sons; yes, we'll be out for Phrynion's blood." Helen's face had turned an ugly shade of purple. She shook her fist.

"Women!" said Theo. "You amaze me, all of you. You know what your brothers will do before they do it. If they needed persuasion, Helen, I don't doubt that you would persuade them."

"It's not difficult, in something as obvious as this." Helen's flush faded. Under Theo's keen glance, she looked embarrassed. "Even without this personal attack, my brothers don't approve of Phrynion's politics. They don't like politics much at all, actually; but they say that no important Athenian family can ignore what's happening in the north. My boys agree. I know without asking that our family will support you, Theo, for the sake of Athens. I know my brothers respect you; they agree with your policies; they won't want you to resign."

"Thank you," said Theo simply.

"Thank you," I chimed in.

"I might say, 'I told you so,'" said Dora to us, "but I won't."

Helen stood up. "Phano, dear granddaughter, I'm sure your head is spinning. I have loved you all your life. If the gods will it, you may learn to love me as well. Now you must sleep. Other people will do what needs to be done. Dora, do you have chamomile in the house? Brew some tea for Phano's nightcap, it calms the nerves."

With her back almost painfully erect, my newfound grandmother marched across the room. In a daze of disbelief, I watched her go, pausing in the doorway to exchange a few more words with Dora. Instead of running away in disgrace, leaving my husband to resign in disgrace, I slept that night in my own dear bed, in my husband's arms. If the gods sent dreams, I did not remember them.

# twenty

The morning plunged us back into anxiety. Battus had come back alone, obeying Dora's orders. He had found no trace of Minta or Newby. "I have put him in charge of a wide search," Dora told us. "He had five helpers last I heard, with more promised. If Newby had just wandered off, Minta would be home by now. Something worse has happened." Her face was gray with fatigue.

"You've been up all night, Mother," said Theo. "We're all worried, but at least Phano and I are rested. You've done so much; go to bed now, and let me take over."

"I will sleep later," said Dora. "I am tired, but we have more to do today than look for a slave and a goose. Helen has been busy too. Her brothers will acknowledge Phano this morning in a public ceremony. Phano, I'll help you get ready; then we must go to the Agora. Helen has sent her own maid to dress your hair."

"Minta will be miserable about that," I said. "No one else can do my hair to suit her, or me either, to tell the truth. Mother, I wish we had some news, I'm sure you're right; something dreadful has happened. If so, Phrynion is behind it."

Dora's chin went up. "Summon your strength, Basilinna," she said. "*You* of all people know better than to accuse a man without proof. We don't know what has happened yet. I'm sorry I said anything. Minta certainly would not want you to worry about her, especially today. This is a great day for all of us."

"It is a great day," I agreed. I stood up straight and proud, as Minta would wish, wherever she might be. "I'm glad of your help, and glad that my grandmother has so much influence in the family of my birth. The least I can do is dress to honor the occasion. Which chiton should I wear?"

I met my great-uncles, Helen's brothers, for the first time in the Agora. They had decided to do everything in the open, where many people could see and hear. The morning sun was not yet high; the air was fresh and cool, easy to breathe even through the linen scarf that partly hid my face. Helen sat on my right side with my father and Mama beside her, and Dora on my left, with Theo. I saw them, and the people jamming the square in front of us, dimly, like shadows. To my relief, Bardian and Nerissa did not appear, but Uncle Nikos's absence saddened me.

Ajax, the older of Helen's brothers, addressed the crowd. "People of Athens," he began, "I am here today to do what is usually done for a babe in arms, a child too young to walk, to acknowledge and welcome a child of our family. Let all citizens of Athens know that Phano, true wife of our Basileus, is the granddaughter of my sister Helen and her husband Cadmus, both citizens of Athens. Her mother, who died when she was born, was Maia, daughter of Helen and Cadmus, and true wife of Stephanos son of Crito, both citizens of Athens.

"Phano's name and ancestry, with the date of her birth, will be entered in our family records. The dowry that would have been her mother's has been paid to her husband for her support. If ever her husband divorces her, that money is for her use. If ever she needs a home, she may claim a home with us."

My mysterious dowry! I turned to Father with raised eyebrows. He blushed.

Uncle Ajax turned to me and held out his hands. I stood. He led me forward and put aside my veil. "All of you here assembled, bear witness."

Surely the gods on high Olympos heard the cheers. I smothered my sniffles. Without my training as Basilinna, I would have dissolved in tears.

After this public ceremony, there was another, with the family members, in the temple of Dionysos. My teacher, the old priestess, poured the libations and burned the sacred herbs. Afterward, she dismissed the others graciously. "A feast waits for you in the courtyard," she told them. "Samian wine, fresh dates and bread, whatever we can offer. Stay as long as you wish." She put her hand on Theo's arm. "King Archon, with your consent, it's urgent I spend some time with your wife."

Theo smiled. "Certainly, Mother. You need not ask. My wife knows she may come to you at any time. It's urgent? When?"

"Now," was the blunt reply. "I hope you will stay to enjoy our hospitality. It may not be convenient for you to wait until we are done, but the Basilinna will be escorted home. Phano, come with me."

I thanked Ajax and the others, hugged Father and Mama, had a quick word with Theo about Minta and Newby, then followed my teacher to her inner room. Two of my priestesses from the festival waited there.

"Say again what you have told me," commanded their superior.

"A woman promised five thousand drachmas if I would take a lover to my bed and then perform my part in the Anthesteria," said one of them.

"A man made me the same offer," said the second. "He wanted to be my lover into the bargain; he said there was another five thousand for him when it was done."

"Lift your eyes," I ordered. "Look at me." I stared at one, then at the other. One woman turned pale; the other blushed brick red; both of them met and held my gaze.

"Did you accept the offer?"

"No."

"Why not?"

"Sacrilege!" said the first woman. "The thought was abomination."

"I saw danger," added the other. "Rightly so. The woman who accepted the money is dead."

"These two came to me, though later than they should have," said the old priestess. "Tell us the rest of it. Who offered that bribe?"

"Reverend Mother, we had no proof."

"Who were they?"

"We believe they were the slaves of a very powerful man."

"His name?"

"Must we repeat it?" Both women were ashy pale.

"You said it once before and lived. The Basilinna will not betray you to him. Say his name."

"Phrynion," they whispered together.

"Phrynion," echoed the old priestess. "Leave us now." She gestured. The two women bowed. They gathered their long black himations to cover even their faces and slipped like shadows through the door. My teacher turned to me. "The fools!" she exclaimed. "They should have come to me at once. Fear palsied them. Well, past's past. We found no proof that would stand up in court, but you may be sure they have it right. Phrynion tried to discredit you right from the start. He told me you would profane the mysteries. That man is your bitter enemy, Phano. Be warned."

I shivered. My mother's family had welcomed me in public that very morning. My husband's family loved me, all but Bardian. My husband was still King Archon of Athens; my father was still his assessor and a member of his board.

And Minta was still missing, along with my pet goose.

"He hid in the sanctuary," I said dully. "He tried to attack me there."

"Phrynion? I know that he did not succeed." The old voice was strong. "You could not have hidden it from me. What happened? You may tell me that; it is permitted."

"Dionysos gave me power. I threw Phrynion off easily. He hit his head and lay behind the altar like a child asleep."

"Or like a body ready for the grave."

"Phrynion will not rest until he has ruined me. Why does he hate me so much? I don't understand."

"He may not hate you at all. He enjoys tormenting you, but he's that kind of person. *Think*, Phano, his motives are clear."

"Is politics enough to account for *everything*? This hatred feels very personal."

"It *is* personal, oh yes. Who is close to you, someone he hates?"

"Mama," I breathed. "Father, because he is her husband."

"Of course. He dislikes your husband as well, I think; that's political, but it's personal too."

"He'll never give up. I'll never be safe."

"Remind yourself of that from time to time, and don't

forget your sacrifices to the gods! The viper may threaten you, Phano, but you can draw its poison."

"The poison of whispers? How can I do that?"

"Don't feel sorry for yourself, girl. Count your friends! How many families supported you this morning? Not to mention this temple! I won't make this sacrilege public, Phano. Even if we could prove everything, I could not keep my priestesses out of it. There would be doubts; future festivals would be damaged.

"I must warn certain people, however, for your safety and ours: two important priests and one other priestess; Bardian, head of Theo's family; Stephanos, your father; Theo, your husband; Ajax, from your mother's family."

"Bardian will never believe you."

"Maybe yes, maybe no; the future will tell. I can start a whispering campaign myself; I'll let him know that. Bardian is too close to your enemy for his own well-being. He must understand that he can't afford to be Phrynion's crony anymore."

"Yesterday I expected to be fleeing from Athens. Today, I am her honored daughter. Even little things make me weep, and your protection is not a little thing, Reverend Mother." I stabbed at my wet cheeks. "I've cried enough tears to make a pond, not a small one. My tunics are never dry."

"Let's think of other things. Stay with me awhile." The old woman laid a wizened paw on my knee, and calmness came to my spirit.

❋

I roused from deep reverie at last. "Dear Mother," I said, "thank you for comforting me. Thank you for teaching me. Thank you for lending me your strength. The gods blessed me when you came into my life."

She smiled with great sweetness. "The blessing was mine also," she assured me.

However long I had been sitting with her, a burden had been lifted from my soul. I wanted to gather up my skirts and run home, singing all the way. Surely the searchers would have found Minta and Newby, and they would be waiting for me. The evening meal would be ready. My stomach rumbled. What with worry and excitement, and maybe pregnancy as well, I'd hardly managed to eat all day. Now I was famished. Before I could reach the door, however, a messenger presented herself. Her face left no doubt that she brought bad news. I braced myself to hear it.

"In—in the courtyard," the woman stammered, "there are many horrid people. Reverend Mother, they say our Basilinna committed sacrilege, and they offer proof." She made the sign to ward off evil. "They demand entrance to the temple. I said they must wait in the courtyard while I speak to you. Come quickly, please."

"Are the others still there?"

"Yes."

"The King Archon as well?"

"He is. Bardian is his relative, is he not? Bardian brings the charge. I am afraid they will come to blows."

"Stay here, Phano, while I see what new villainy your

enemies have hatched." The old priestess could still move fast.

I followed, apologizing for my disobedience. I could not cool my heels while my fate hung in the balance. Whatever waited, I had to face it now.

# twenty-one

The late-afternoon sun no longer shone into the courtyard, but the day had not yet faded. Bardian stood with his back to us. Theo, Father, Mama and the rest faced him, mouths agape, bodies frozen in shock. Bardian's smug voice was the only sound.

"Ajax, you'll regret moving so fast," Bardian said. "It's a pity your invitation reached me too late to stop you. That's what comes of listening to a woman."

"I don't regret acknowledging the Basilinna," said Ajax. His face was red with anger. "She was born into our family. We should have acknowledged it years ago. No matter what you might have said, today you could not have stopped me. Furthermore, I strongly resent your insinuations. Phano was born to our family, but she now belongs to yours. You have a duty to protect her; I should hardly need to remind you of it."

"I have a duty to protect our family," Bardian replied. All attention was focused on him and Ajax, mine too, but now my gaze widened, and I saw my enemy. Phrynion stood well back in the shadows. As if he felt me watching him, he turned his head toward me. Even without a good view of his face, I sensed his pleasure in the ugly scene.

The tiny movement alerted Bardian, who pivoted to face us. My teacher, chief priestess of Dionysos, gathered authority around her like a mantle. I stood behind her and to one side, recalling how she had trained me, reminding myself that I was not an unimportant girl. I was the Basilinna, Savior of Athens.

We stood silently for three long breaths before the priestess spoke. "This is unseemly behavior in the courtyard of a sacred temple," she said. "Bardian, I hear that you and your friends tried to push your way into the sacred place. Phano may or may not have been guilty of anything, but you came within breathing distance of sacrilege yourself."

"Honored Mother, high priestess of Dionysos," said Bardian, "it was my painful duty to bring new evidence about the whore's daughter before you immediately. Along with her mother and Stephanos, she has deceived us all. She went through a form of marrying into our family, but it was all lies. A marriage based on deceit is no marriage at all. My nephew Theo will have to divorce her at once. He will also have to repay her dowry, Ajax; we won't try to keep it; it does not belong to us. I'm sorry I spoke out of turn about your actions today. You were taken in as much as we were; I'll see you don't lose by it."

"Enough of this." The high priestess's voice was colder than winter ice. "Your tongue trips gleefully ahead of you, Bardian. Have you favored the company with any account of this evidence you speak of? It should have been reported to me decently, in private, with time for a thorough investigation; but decency is past hoping for now. What you have said so loudly here will be repeated throughout Athens. Now let's have the rest of it, in front of everyone. I know Phano. I am well schooled to recognize deceit—or sacrilege—and never has my nose detected the slightest scent of either. No. The air in this courtyard has lost its usual sweetness, but not because the Basilinna stands with me here."

Bardian had turned brick red long before she had finished. I thought Dionysos might strike him where he stood, but lightning is the weapon of Father Zeus. The ways of the god of the vine are different. Bardian was silent, but another man came forward to kneel respectfully at the old priestess's feet: Bouly's father.

"Reverend Mother, may I speak? Be certain, I take no pleasure in it."

"You may speak."

"I hate this," he said, "but we have all been deceived. Phano herself has been deceived, I am certain. She has been my daughter's friend; I have talked to her frequently.

Like you, Reverend Mother, I have found her honest and trustworthy, even though no proper Athenian can believe she has been well brought up. When this new information came to my attention, I myself investigated it.

"I have spoken with the midwife who delivered Stephanos's baby, and who cared for the child's mother until she died. Maia died of smallpox. The midwife caught the illness too."

"My mother," I said, using the same words that Ajax had spoken that morning: "My mother was Maia, daughter of Helen and Cadmus, and true wife of Stephanos son of Crito, both citizens of Athens. She died in giving birth to me."

"You believe this, but it is not true," he said. "Nera was your mother. Maia died of smallpox when you were very tiny. The same midwife was present three days later when Maia's baby died. It wasn't you, Phano. Maia's baby had a birthmark on her cheek. Your face is clean." Bouly's father stood up. He looked away from me. "Bring the witness," he said.

There was a short delay; then a female figure, cloaked in some dark fabric, heavily veiled, stepped forward. She put back her veil. Her face was pitted with smallpox scars. Minta and Mama too had told me that my mother died in giving birth. If I had not been born, I reasoned, she would not have died. Now it seemed I had not killed her after all. Smallpox must be a horrible way to die.

Whose daughter would I be when everything was revealed?

"Were you present at Maia's death?" asked the priestess.

"I was the midwife," she replied. "Maia died of smallpox. Her mother, whom I see here, knows this; so does her husband, Stephanos. Ask them."

"It is the reason we were not with her when she died," Helen said. "It seems very selfish now, letting her die alone."

"She did not die alone," said the midwife. "I was with her. The baby might have lived if her father had found a wet nurse to take her. She spewed up goat's milk as fast as I dripped it into her mouth. My own fever came on soon after her death, poor little mite. The slave had orders to take the body to her father for burial."

"Who was the slave?"

"Her name was Minta. She came with Maia from her parents' home."

"Minta is here," said Bouly's father. "She is a reluctant witness, but she cannot deny the truth."

Somehow I knew, even before two more men dragged something—someone—out of the deepest shadows. The sun was gone now, and the day fading rapidly. "We will have light before we continue," said the priestess. "Bring torches."

The silent air was heavy, so heavy I could barely breathe. Priestesses came and stood about us with burning torches. The gloomy courtyard sprang into flickering light.

When the men tried to stand her on her feet, Minta

fell, sprawling in the dirt. I cried out, but the priestess hushed me with her hand.

"Bring a stool for this woman," she commanded, "no, bring a chair with a back, and a cup of wine, and water to wash her face."

"A chair for a slave?" said Bardian contemptuously. "And wine? You surprise me, Mother."

The priestess did not reply. She herself lifted Minta's chin, and washed the poor bruised face. Her hands held the wine to Minta's lips.

"She has confirmed the midwife's story," said Bardian. "Ask her, let her tell you."

"Is it so?" I asked, numb with grief.

"I took the baby to her father," Minta whispered.

"Hush, Phano." The priestess's voice was tender, more a caress than a rebuke. "You took the baby's body to Stephanos, is that correct? Speak louder, Minta, if you can."

"This is a lie." Father spoke now, for the first time.

"Later, please," said the priestess. "Do not interrupt this witness."

"You expect a slave to tell the truth?" asked Bardian. "Beat her again first."

"She has been tortured," the priestess said.

"Fifty blows. How else do you get truth from a slave?" said Bardian. "The laws of Athens call for torture before a slave gives evidence."

"I know the laws of Athens," said the priestess. "I will have silence, all of you, and no more talk of beating. Now,

206

Minta, you are outside the temple of Dionysos. Inside that door, the place is sacred. Answer me now as if you stood on sacred ground. I will know if you speak the truth."

"I took the baby," Minta gasped. "The midwife believed she was dead, but she was too sick herself to know. I nursed the baby, and she lived. My mistress Phano is that child. This is the truth, I swear it."

"That's not what you said before." Bardian's face was purple now, not red.

"What I said earlier, that the baby died, that was a lie. You were bound to have that answer from me; no other would content you. I did not give it quickly, as you know," Minta said despairingly. "I kept telling myself that I might someday tell the truth if I lived; I could never tell it if I died."

"I have never seen a birthmark on Phano's cheek," the priestess observed.

"Not that cheek," said Minta.

The priestess turned to me, her eyebrows raised.

"On my left buttock," I told her, feeling the flush mount into my face.

"I can confirm that," Theo said. His face relaxed slightly; a hint of a smile touched his mouth.

"And I," Mama added.

"Ah," said the priestess. "Thank you, King Archon. Thank you, Nera. In another matter, I would take your word, but this I must see with my own eyes. I am not the only one who should witness it. Your grandmother, your great-uncle, your uncle by marriage, your friend's father should all see this mark with their own eyes. The place will be private, but we will do this before anyone leaves. We must destroy this vicious lie about Phano once and for all."

"Then let us be thorough." Mama spoke. "Examine me too. It will not embarrass me. Any woman who has given birth carries marks on her body. There are none on mine. I have never borne a child."

"We will witness Phano's birthmark," said the priestess, "and Nera's body as well, for confirmation, and so that we can speak with absolute conviction, from our own personal knowledge. However, none of us doubts what we will find.

"Bardian, you have wronged Phano; you have wanted to believe evil of her; you have intended harm to her, and you *have* harmed her. I have heard that your father does not speak or move; however, he still breathes. Today you speak as head of your family, but your father's life thread has not yet been cut. He would not be the first man to return from the shores where Charon waits. How would he look on your stewardship of the family honor?

"That's not all. Your offense clearly goes beyond the personal. In harming the Basilinna, you have threatened harm to Athens. You had best think what amends you can make to your nephew and his wife."

Bardian's face had been many colors that day; now it was bloodless, white. "I was duped," he said dully. "The man who duped me is an expert. Many others have been fooled."

"I am one of them," said Bouly's father. "Phano, I should have trusted my daughter. Her instincts about people have always been good. Bouly will rejoice to hear this news. Theo, you and I have had political differences. Those differences may have clouded my judgment. I believed a man's lies about Phano. I believed the same man about politics: more lies, do you think? I will reevaluate my position." He would have continued, but the priestess raised her hand, and he stopped.

While the two men spoke, Phrynion had backed up against the courtyard wall and begun to edge toward the gate. Bardian suddenly turned to look for him. "Where are you, Phrynion?" he yelled. "Running away again? Come here and join us, as you deserve. Don't think you can escape."

Bouly's father moved quickly to stand by the gate. My husband joined him there. Phrynion, seeing his way blocked, walked slowly toward me, the priestess, Bardian and the chair where Minta sat. His fists were balled in a way that I knew well, his right hand near the hilt of a nasty-looking knife.

"Gentlemen, enough!" The priestess's voice carried an edge of anger. "You try my patience too far. Phrynion, you may not enter this temple or any other holy place in Athens again. I will send word of this decree to the high priests of the other deities of High Olympos, along with something of the reasons for it. Your presence would defile any temple, and risk bringing a god's anger upon the city. Be warned; do not try to enter."

"Am I to be convicted with no trial? I care for Athens as much as anyone." Phrynion glared viciously at me. "Are you telling me the whore's daughter has won?"

"Silence! Be silent, or you shall be silenced at my command!" Tension thrummed between them. The priestess recovered more quickly. Her voice was slower as she continued. "Phrynion, you will be watched. Every time you eat or drink, go into the streets or to the Agora, every time you exchange a sentence with anyone, you will be watched. Every breath, be assured that someone is counting it.

"You are suspected of dealings with Philip of Macedon, of taking his money to betray Athens. If ever proof is found, it will be used against you. If you remain in Athens, your life will not be pleasant. If you attack Phano, or this temple, it will be short. All of us gathered here have long memories, and those who come after us will have long memories.

"Now, begone."

She turned and led the way to her private room, where we had sat together a few hours earlier. Helen's servants carried Minta's chair, while Helen herself held the wine cup to Minta's swollen mouth.

We crowded into the small room. Theo held me against him, hiding my hot face; his hand adjusted my clothes while the others lined up to witness my red strawberry birthmark. Mama was silent when her turn came and her body was bared to them. I did not watch while they examined her, though from the shocked exclamations, the observers did not fail to see the angry scars where Phrynion's men had beaten her.

"Thank you, Nera," said the priestess at last. "Thank you, Phano. Minta, you have my gratitude and my respect."

The temple scribe had squatted patiently inside the door, his writing case at his side. "Take your Egyptian papyrus," the priestess commanded, "and oak-gall ink, the best you have. Write as I say." Quickly, the scribe put down the facts: I, Phano, was Maia's daughter, as shown by the midwife and by Minta. Further, I could not possibly be Nera's daughter, as Nera had never borne a child. My birthmark and Nera's body, observed in person by all the signatories, had confirmed these facts.

The priestess was the first to sign this document, followed by Theo, Bardian, Ajax, Father and everybody else. Minta refused to leave until she had seen everyone sign the papyrus and made her own mark at the end, though her hand trembled and she left a huge inkblot.

When all was completed, Theo picked Minta up and carried her in his own arms, with me beside him, to the gates, where Battus waited with a litter to take her battered body home.

# twenty-two

I slept late the next day. Theo was gone from my side when I woke, but Dora rose from a stool and brought me chamomile tea. I sipped it as I padded over to check on Minta, snoring lightly on her narrow bed. Theo had moved it into our room when we brought her home the night before. Mama had sent her own special salve, which I had applied gently to the wounds on Minta's poor back. Her body was a mass of cuts and bruises, but there seemed to be no broken bones.

"May Hera preserve me from another day like yesterday," said Dora. "I'd rather watch a drama than be part of it, and I was only one of the chorus, not a major player. You were splendid, Phano. I admire you tremendously, but I'm also concerned for my grandchild, to say nothing of his mother. Do let's have a quiet day."

A quiet day was exactly what I wanted. "Minta has cared for me all my life," I said. "Today I shall care for her. If we find Newby safe and sound, I'll ask for nothing more."

Much to my surprise, Father arrived later that morning. A slave followed him, carrying Newby. Her legs and beak were tied, the knots pulled cruelly tight. Father held her, squawking and struggling, while I cut the ropes. He came with me while I took Newby back to her nest. The hen had been dismissed. The eggs were warm, but Newby refused to settle. I coaxed her, but she followed me as soon as I turned to leave. At last, I retrieved the indignant hen and all of us, Father, Newby and I, went up to sit with Minta. Newby inspected every corner of the room, honking and squawking. At last she drank and ate. "Will she be all right?" I asked.

Minta propped herself up on an elbow, smiling while she watched. "I think so," she whispered. "Give her time."

"Minta, your teeth!" Her mouth showed a gap like Mama's. "Was that Phrynion's work?"

"Yes," she said, "but I'll heal. It's good to be home."

"I was afraid you were dead, Minta," I told her. "I won't be scared like that again. My home will be yours as long as you wish—all your life, I hope—but it will be home to a free woman, not a slave. Theo and I agreed about this last night; he is having the documents prepared. No one shall torture you again and claim justification under the law because you are a slave."

Minta cried, I hugged her, too hard; she groaned, Newby squawked and we all laughed. It was not exactly a quiet day after all, but none of us complained. Father had to tell us how he came to have Newby, and a strange tale it was.

"We're lucky she's alive," he said. "Phrynion's servants took the goose, hoping to get their hands on Minta. You guessed right about that; it worked too. I suppose he put off killing Newby in case he needed her again. Who knows what would have happened except for Bardian!"

"Bardian? Father, this isn't a time for teasing."

"I don't trust him one iota," Father said, "but he brought the goose to me, trussed as you found her. He told me he had taken her from Phrynion's pens. He did not bring her to you in person, being unsure of his welcome."

"I can certainly believe *that*!" Dora spoke acidly. "Nobody values family members more highly than I do, but Bardian tries my patience sorely. How I wish that Nikos would recover!"

"I wish Mama and I could care for him. I worry about dear Uncle Nikos. Theo has visited him, but Theo couldn't stay long, and he has no skills as a healer; nor has Nerissa or anyone else in that house. Mama and I should be tending the old man."

"Phano, are you sure you should do that?" Dora sounded worried.

"Don't fret, Mother," I told her, "I'll take care of myself as well."

"I doubt Bardian would object now," said Father drily. "The high priestess ordered him to make amends. I'll be your messenger to him, if you wish. If this works out, Theo will be delighted; it would go a long way toward healing rifts in our families."

❋

Bardian came to call the following afternoon. Theo arrived in time to warn me to change my clothes and alert the kitchen. "If anyone had predicted that my uncle would call here to ask a favor, I would have told him to stop dreaming," he said. "Wonders will never cease. Phano, my revered uncle is deeply concerned about his father's health. He asks—no, he begs, he pleads—for you to come and nurse the old man. Bardian did not send a messenger; he came himself to see me, and he is coming in person to speak to you. When he left me, he was on the way to ask Stephanos if Nera can help too."

"Mama would rather he asked *her*."

"Stephanos will tell him the same; and he'll do it; wait and see."

I laughed. "The gods can work great wonders. See, out of Phrynion's evil plot comes the promise of something good."

"Are you sure it won't be too much for you?" asked Theo.

"I'm fine," I assured him. "I've fretted about Uncle Nikos. Caring for him will help me too."

215

"I'm glad. If Uncle Nikos is not too close to the Underworld, you and Nera may yet pull him back."

I don't know if Bardian was more uncomfortable, or if I was. His visit was brief and formal, as satisfactory as it could be in the circumstances. He apologized for behaving badly to me. He almost went so far as to ask me to forgive him, but pulled back just short of anything so humbling. He asked me to care for his father, beginning as soon as possible. Mama had already agreed.

That is how Theo and I, along with Stephanos and Mama, came to have our evening meal at Bardian's home. I had braced myself to endure noise, but the pig-children were dining with friends; we could hear ourselves speak. The food was delicious. So much meat! Theo and I usually had meat with our dinner at noon. After years of lentil stew, meat once a day was luxury. Here, with the evening meal, there were two meat dishes: a stew, as well as platters of tiny quail, along with their eggs, and quantities of everything. I tried to eat, so that Bardian would not feel insulted, but I stopped the servants from refilling my plate. Eventually Theo rescued me.

"It's a shame not to linger over this fine meal," he said, "but my wife is eager to see her patient. May I take Phano up to Uncle Nikos? And you as well, Nera, if you're ready? I won't stay with you, except to see you settled. Bardian and I, and Nerissa, will be here if you need us."

Bardian and Nerissa knew that at least one of them should go with us. It was almost comical to see their struggle between food and good manners. In the end, both of them chose food. "If you're sure you'll be all right," muttered Bardian.

"You'll find a slave by his bed," said Nerissa. "Someone is with him constantly. Whatever you need, just let us know." She sighed. "Father's condition has been a strain, you understand. You are taking a huge burden from me. Pardon me if I stay here; I haven't eaten a decent meal for a week."

With a lamp in his hand, Theo led the way into the courtyard and up the nearer flight of stairs to a half-open door. He waved me and Mama ahead. The room was dark, though one dim light flickered, and I walked cautiously toward it. Not cautiously enough! My sandaled toe bumped against some piece of furniture, and I gasped with pain. Theo pushed past me with his lamp. I glimpsed a white-covered bed; then he moved the lamp to show a chair beside it. A woman lifted her close-cropped dark head and rubbed sleep from her eyes. "Stand up, slave," Theo roared. "Is this how you do your duty? Get out, and don't come near this room again."

The woman seemed to shrink before our eyes. She crept toward the door. I lifted her face as she passed so that I would know her again, with her sallow skin, sharp chin and sullen eyes. Maybe some slaves should be whipped.

I had stumbled against a sleeping couch. I pushed it clear and went to stand beside Theo, looking down at the big bed. Mama followed me. At first I thought Uncle Nikos wasn't there. Then I looked again and saw his head, his face like a skull, the slight bulge in the coverlet that concealed his body.

Mama put her fingers on Uncle Nikos's throat. She counted under her breath. She held one hand, then the other, gently squeezing and releasing each in turn. "Squeeze my fingers if you can," she said. His hands were translucent, like wax. They did not move. Mama pushed the blue-veined eyelids apart and stared into the faded blue eyes, first the right, then the left. "Blink if you can hear me," she told him. Uncle Nikos did not blink.

Mama gestured to me, and we turned him over. I think he did not weigh much more than the birds we had been eating. Then Mama tried to remove his linen under-tunic. "It's stuck to his backside," she said grimly. "Theo, tell the slaves to bring hot water and salt, and plenty of clean, dry cloths. You might as well go back to dinner. This won't be a pretty sight."

I gasped in horror as we soaked off the cloth. Our patient's wrinkled buttocks were a mass of blisters; many of them had burst. Bardian and Nerissa, along with Theo, appeared just as Mama and I finished settling him for the night. His sores were bandaged; his clothing and bed linen were clean. He lay on his right side, facing us. His eyes were open, but there was no life in them. Indeed, the only sound of life was what we had heard all the time: slow, rasping breaths, in and, after a silent pause, out again.

"Why is my father curled up like that?" Bardian demanded. He sounded unpleasantly like his usual arrogant self.

"Let me show you." Mama beckoned to them. She

raised the coverlet and lifted the clothing from a bony hip. Very gently, she unwrapped a small bandage. Mama and I had cleaned the oozing sores. Now the exposed flesh was raw but clean. Blood seeped from the edges of the wound. "All his backside is like this," said Mama quietly. "If he can feel anything, he has been in agony. I don't understand why the doctor did not insist on nurses to care for him."

Nerissa turned away. "I don't know how you can look at him, let alone touch him. I could not." She shuddered. "I ordered the slaves to keep him clean and fed. They assured me he could not swallow; there was nothing to be done. The doctor said the same."

"He has gone far on his way to the Underworld," Mama agreed. "I fear we won't be able to draw him back. Certainly, Phano and I can make him more comfortable. I should like two slaves outside the door, ready for my orders. Right now, I want warm milk in one bowl and chicken broth in another. I want good olive oil to rub into his skin. Old Charon and I have a longstanding feud. Many a passenger has been almost ready to board the ferry in the land of the dead, but I've pulled him back, and the ferryman has had to wait, for days, or months, sometimes for years. We all take that ride, but not before our time if I can help it."

"Thank you, Nera," said Nerissa.

"Thank you, Phano." Bardian's voice was as stiff as his shoulders.

"Thank you for allowing us to help." As I closed the door behind them, I hoped my own voice was as stiff as his.

Theo drew me into his arms. "This is horrible," he

said. "I blame myself. I sat by him and held his hand, but I never looked under the covers. How could I be so stupid? Now you are here and it's too late."

"It might have been too late anyhow," I said, though I was angry with him myself. *When you sat beside him, where was your nose?* I wanted to ask. I had taken the pus-filled clothing to be burned, and I still felt sick with the smell of it.

"Don't waste energy blaming yourself, Theo," said Mama. "You had the affairs of Athens on your mind. Let me tell you now what I expect.

"I think your uncle won't rally. Don't expect any last words from him. He may live for a week or only for a day or two. It will depend on how much milk and broth Phano and I can get him to take. He will be weaker every day. He gives no sign of pain, but no sign of anything else, so I can't be sure. All my experience tells me this family will be holding a funeral before two weeks have passed.

"Let's be practical. Do you want Bardian to know this now or later? How will Uncle Nikos's death affect you and Phano? These are the questions you must think about, but you need not answer them tonight. Go home and sleep. Phano and I will take turns to watch and rest."

When I tried to spoon broth into Uncle Nikos's slack mouth, it all ran out again. Mama could do no better. In the end, we did what one would do for a motherless baby when no wet nurse could be found: sopped up liquid with a clean rag and squeezed it into his mouth, drop by drop. At first we had to keep turning his head sideways so that he would not choke. After a while, however, his throat convulsed, once, then again, and he swallowed. Mama rested then, and roused later to take her turn while I slept. Much to my surprise, I felt calm and rested in the morning, and dear Uncle Nikos did not look so dreadfully like an unburied corpse.

We began our day quietly, taking turns with broth and milk. "I should be feeling sad," I told Mama, "but I'm not. This is so peaceful. What's wrong with me? Uncle Nikos is dying, and I only want to go on sitting beside him dripping soup into his mouth. On and on and on."

Mama laughed. "When was the last time you could sit and be at peace?" she asked. "Can you remember? Not since you started preparing for the festival, I'm sure of that. Perhaps, in his deep dreams, Uncle Nikos knows you are caring for him. Perhaps he knows that your shoulders are relaxed, that your whole body is relaxed, for the first time in many months. Nothing would please him more."

"You and I are together," I told her. "That pleases *me.* Dora has welcomed me as a daughter, and I've had Minta, but dear Mama, I've missed you very much."

"Nobody to remind you to be practical?" Mama's gaptoothed grin made me want to hug her.

"Nobody to laugh with when Theo is at work, as he is most of the time, and anyway, Mama, nobody is more fun than you."

"There's not much fun in me these days," said Mama quietly. "I have plenty to eat, a home, a husband who loves me, everything a practical person like me could want, even if there is also a shortage of fun. The gods have been generous; I know it and give thanks." She shrugged. "This good time won't last, of course, everything changes."

"Mama," I said, "you mustn't talk like that. We'll see more of each other from now on, won't we? That will be a good change. There is another good change coming, a very good change." I paused, just as Mama would do, for drama.

To my relief, Mama's eyes sparkled. "This sounds interesting," she said. "Tell me more, or must I guess?"

I might have teased her, but I couldn't have her waiting another minute. I patted my belly. She knew at once; her face was radiant.

"The baby will need a grandmama who knows how to have fun," I told her.

We tended Uncle Nikos and talked about the baby, dividing our morning between the soon-to-die and the not-yet-born, death and life flowing together. Toward noon I picked up my neglected spindle and began to feed the wool from my basket. Soon I felt the yarn once more, fine and even under my hand. Dear Theo had bought me a new thigh shield. It was plain white clay, not truly comfortable, but I intended to get used to it.

The day was interrupted three times. Bardian and Nerissa both looked in, exclaimed over our patient's improvement and left again. The doctor did the same. "Don't criticize him," Mama warned me. "It won't help."

Theo sat with us in the evening. I wrung warm milk into the open mouth, and Uncle Nikos swallowed.

"Could you be wrong, Nera?" my husband asked hopefully. "He looks so much better today."

"No," said Mama quietly. "A week, maybe, that's the best you can expect."

Phrynion had not entered my mind all day, nor had I worried about the fire of vicious rumor he had lit and fanned, until Theo came. Perhaps Mama can't really read my mind. Maybe it's more that we often think the same things at the same time. Mama spoke first. "Tell us, Theo, what do you hear about Phrynion? Has he run away from Athens yet?"

"My officers tell me he's not been seen in the Agora," Theo replied, "but as of today, he had not left Athens. The high priestess is wise and powerful, but Ajax and I decided there would be no harm in adding our threats and promises to hers. We went with witnesses to Phrynion's home this morning.

" 'I am here to inform you officially before these witnesses that Phano is my niece's daughter,' Ajax said. 'She has been publicly acknowledged as a member of my family. She is a citizen of Athens through her father and mother both.'

" 'I am here to inform you before these witnesses that I intend to sue you for slander,' I said. 'I might postpone my suit if I do not hear the slander about my wife's birth again. If I hear it, I will assume it came from you.'

" 'If Theo decides to sue you, I will join him,' Ajax said."

"What did Phrynion say about that?"

"No words, but if a look could pierce a man's heart, I'd have died on the spot. We've got him, haven't we? Phrynion is finished in this city."

"Don't count on it." Mama sounded like my dear old priestess. Even better, she sounded like her old self. "He'll be planning more mischief. It's our job to think what it might be and to be ready for him, or better, to plan an attack of our own. I'll put my mind to it."

# twenty-three

As it turned out, we had no chance to put our minds to it. Events moved too fast. Early next morning, Mama and I were bathing our patient's sores. They were starting to scab over, a good sign. "His breathing isn't so noisy," I noted. "That's good, isn't it?"

"That's good, Phano," Mama agreed. Something in her voice made me wonder how she meant it: Uncle Nikos might be sinking more quickly. I did not ask.

"Shhh! Listen!" I put my finger to my lips. Mama and I stared at each other. "That's the gate," I whispered. "Who could possibly be calling so early?" I stepped out onto the wide balcony and peered over the railing, looking down at the courtyard below. That chariot, I knew it! I knew the balding squatty man climbing down. I didn't need to see his face.

*Ah, Hera help me, I must not faint!* I forced myself to edge back from the railing, back into the room. The gods in Olympos be thanked, he did not look up.

Mama's strong arms came round me, partly leading, partly carrying me to the narrow bed by the door. "Lie down, Phano," she commanded. "Don't try to talk. Drink a little water." She held the cup to my lips, then tucked a warm blanket around me.

"I'm all right, Mama," I told her. "Let me sit up."

"Hmph," said Mama, but she fetched pillows for my back. "Now, what ghost did you see? That was our enemy down there, am I right? Phrynion?"

"Yes."

In my mind, I was back in the little sanctuary; Phrynion had thrown me down and was ready to force himself on me. The sight of him was enough to bring it all back, even the putrid smell of his rotten teeth.

"You'd better tell me about it," Mama said quietly.

So I did.

"That's my good girl," Mama murmured. She rocked me like a baby. I had told the old priestess and never shed a single tear. Now I cried and cried. When it was over, I felt clean again. "He did not succeed," said Mama. "Remind yourself of that. The god gave you strength, and you fought him off. That's important. Even if he had forced you, though, he has no power over you except what you give him. Just now, you let the sight of him make you faint. Don't do that again. Summon your anger. You have the stink of him in your nostrils, don't you? Disgusting man!" Her eyes narrowed. "Have you told Theo about this?"

"No, Mama." I wanted to tell my husband, and I didn't want to. The day itself had not been the right time. I had been full of the power of the god; when that power passed, I was exhausted. No time since then had seemed any better.

"Don't tell him. He sees Phrynion clearly enough; better than through a haze of anger. For the sake of Athens, Theo can't afford to be obsessed with a single enemy. Did you tell the old priestess?"

"I told her. She knew I spoke the truth; there was no sacrilege. Mama, do you hear shouting down in the courtyard?"

Again we listened.

"I hear an argument," said Mama. "A noisy argument. Rude, tut-tut. Two men, do you agree? It's just as well that Phrynion does not know we are here."

"Maybe he does. Maybe that's what they are arguing about."

"Shall I see if I can hear them?" Mama started toward the balcony. She almost collided with Nerissa at the door.

"Forgive me, Nera, I'm so frightened." Nerissa's face was scarlet; her jowls quivered, her whole enormous body shook as she lowered herself onto a couch. "That villain! We'll be ruined, we're lost." She burst into great gulping sobs. Her huge breasts shook like puddings.

"Calm yourself, Nerissa. Now!" Mama's voice was a

whip, but Nerissa went on wailing. Mama took the bowl of water from the washstand and threw it in her face. That stopped her; she stared at us with her mouth open.

Mama tossed a towel. Nerissa's sausage arms came up and caught it. "Dry your face. Good. I take it you weren't in the same room, but close enough to hear them when they talked. It's nothing to blush for; they were not whispering. Tell us, maybe we can help."

Mama's last statement set Nerissa off again. "Nobody can help, we're ruined, we're lost." Before we could calm her, the door opened once more.

"Remind me to ask for a bar on that door," Mama muttered.

Bardian stood in the doorway. His face was white and soggy, like unbaked dough. "Get up, Wife," he said. "You have no business here." His voice sagged like his body. All the bluster had evaporated.

Nerissa levered herself upright. She plodded out behind her husband, their steps heavy and flat crossing the balcony and descending the stairs.

"Why didn't he come five minutes later?" I said. "We'd have had the whole story. Now we have nothing."

"Not exactly," said Mama. "Bring that milk and a fresh cloth." We sat on each side of our patient. "What did Nerissa say? Her words, please."

" 'I'm so frightened. That villain. We'll be ruined.' "

"Yes," Mama agreed, wringing milk into Uncle Nikos's mouth, "and also, 'We're lost.' "

"Bardian was frightened too, wasn't he?" I added.

"Oh yes, no doubt about it."

"We know who the villain is: Phrynion." I began to feel excited. "How could Phrynion ruin them? What threat could he make?"

"A family matter, or money, or politics," said Mama. "It must be one of those three, or more than one."

"They tried the family matter," I said grimly. "Me. They agreed about that, however. If Theo divorced me, it wouldn't damage Bardian; everybody knew he had not welcomed me."

"Let's try the other two," said Mama.

"Money. If Bardian lent a lot of money, and Phrynion refused to pay it back."

"I have a nose for money problems," said Mama. "There's no smell of it here. Remember, Bardian was ready to send back your dowry. It must be political."

"Phrynion has been taking bribes from Philip of Macedon." I began slowly, but this line of deduction felt *right*. "He is a traitor to Athens. If that were made public, in a way that would be believed, Phrynion would be ruined. Bardian too, if he is part of it."

"The threat is the same, whether he is part of it or not. Bardian loves to be the center of attention; he has spoken publicly time and again for the rich men's party. Phrynion has pushed him forward as the leader. If Phrynion's treachery is exposed, nobody will believe that Bardian is not up to his armpits in the plot."

"Theo must know right away," I said. "This is *our* family."

"Of course," Mama agreed. "Certainly we must talk to Theo."

Our messenger returned without my husband, however, and with only the briefest of messages from him. The archons of Athens were meeting. Emissaries from Thebes were about to join them. Meetings might continue for several days. He would see us when he could.

The messenger was a trusted slave; he had been my husband's *pedagogos* when he was a child, and now worked in his office, not our household. "What did my husband say?" I asked him.

"Yours was the second urgent message from this house today," the man replied. "The master said, 'Tell them to let me know if there's a death in the family.'" His eyes flickered to the slight figure on the bed, then back again. "'Otherwise, whatever it is, they must cope as best they can.'"

"Tell your master not to worry," I said. "This is nothing; we can do what's needed." But I added to Mama as the door swung shut behind him, "I only wish I knew what that might be."

"It's a pity Bardian has such a low opinion of women," said Mama. "But we won't change that in a hurry. He wants to talk to Theo too, and he can't. Let's try to reach Stephanos. Bardian doesn't like him, but he's close to Theo, and he's a man."

"He may be with Theo."

"He may be at home."

Stephanos had not arrived, however, nor had we heard

from him, when Dora and Helen knocked on the door. "Mother. Grandmother." Warm hugs from both of them. I looked anxiously at Mama.

"Enjoy your family, Phano," she laughed. "It won't put my nose out of joint. Love is love. We can never have too much of it."

"You are part of our family too, Nera." Dora put her arms around Mama. Helen hesitated a moment, then did the same.

Mama had been so quick with her words only a moment ago. Now she was speechless, blinking back tears. "I never thought to see this day," she said. "Don't worry, Helen, I won't rush out to tell all your friends that you hugged a courtesan."

"Tell them if you like," said Helen. "It's a surprise to me as well, I won't say it's not, but you've done well by our girl here, and you are my son-in-law's wife."

Dora sat beside Uncle Nikos. She lifted his limp hand and cradled it. "Theo told us how you found him," she said. "I have been a visitor too, like Theo, and I did not see what was needed. It hurt me dreadfully to look at him, here but not here, you know. I think I tried not to see. Thank you, Phano. If you had not persisted, neither of you would have been here to help. Thank you, Nera, from my heart. Can I do something for him now?"

I gave her the bowl of broth and a fresh cloth, and she took her turn wringing drops of soup into his mouth. Mama sat across from her.

I picked up my spindle. Helen set her stool beside

mine. "Did you ever have a different thigh shield?" she asked. "With little birds inside a wreath?"

My hands trembled. "It was yours, Grandmother. I broke it."

"Accidents happen to all of us. You liked it, then."

"It was no accident. I loved it, and I smashed it in a rage. A thousand times I've wished the moment back again." Helen said nothing. Nor did I. After some minutes, I went on with my work.

Nerissa sent servants with food, platters of dates and figs, fresh bread and honey and a jug of well-watered wine. She herself appeared soon after. Servants brought more stools. Everyone moved quietly, but the room, which had easily accommodated a big bed, a narrow one, plus a chair and stool, was suddenly very crowded. "I don't suppose he notices," said Nerissa uncertainly.

"I don't suppose he does," Mama agreed. "Is your husband feeling better?"

"Probably not," said Nerissa. "Theo sent him away with some excuse. He wouldn't see his uncle, even for a minute. Bardian is in his room. He's probably getting drunk."

"If it will make him feel better, my husband had no time for me either," I said.

Nerissa waved her arm, as if to say it didn't matter.

"Theo is a sensible man," said Theo's mother. "You know he has his reasons." She stood up. "Thank you for this feast, Nerissa. Helen and I should leave now; we have stayed far too long."

Helen scrambled to her feet. "Of course. Perhaps we can come again tomorrow. Nerissa. Nera, Phano dear."

The next arrival did not trip over Dora and Helen, although Nerissa was still seated on her stool when he arrived: my father. Nerissa seemed to be in a daze. In her left hand, she held the date she had picked up when she first sat down. To my amazement, she had not put it, or any other food, into her mouth.

Father and Mama hugged and held each other. As always, I felt that little surge of power; the connection crackled between them. "I can't stay long," Father began. "The fate of Athens may be decided today. It's my job to put information together, to be ready when the archons need it. Theo and I know that you have a crisis here. Tell me about it, quickly. I'll help if I can."

As Mama and I explained, Nerissa's blank expression began to fade. She popped the date into her mouth, then crammed in half a dozen more, spitting out the pits and talking at the same time. "Phrynion will ruin us," she said. "There's nothing to be done. Take a drink with Bardian, Stephanos, you'll see. He has wanted to be head of the family for so long—not that he ever wanted his father to die, just that he longed to be head. His wish will come true about the same time as his disgrace. The gods are cruel to us." She jammed another handful of dates into her mouth.

"This threat is connected to Philip of Macedon," said Mama. "Phano and I are sure of it."

"In that case, I'd best take some wine with Bardian."

Father stood and bowed gallantly. "This problem, whatever it is, may tie in with our business in the city."

Father did not quite run down the stairs, but he moved surprisingly fast. A short time later, an unfamiliar chariot appeared in the courtyard. Bardian staggered out to it and clambered up. Father gave him a push. Then Father mounted, took the reins, and touched his whip to the horse's backs. They did not return.

"I'm going to bed," Nerissa told us at last. "My slaves will bring your food." She moved like an old woman, bent under a load almost too heavy to bear.

Bardian did not appear on the following day, nor was there any message for us. Dora and Helen dropped by in the afternoon, to check on Uncle Nikos and see if we had word from Theo or Bardian or anyone else. All the important men in Athens were at the meeting, it seemed. "Nobody knows anything," said Helen angrily. "Even the slaves don't know. It's unbelievable." By bedtime, Nerissa, Mama and I were worried. If Mama and I had not been so busy with Uncle Nikos, we'd have been frantic. The old man grew weaker, his breathing more labored, his swallowing more hesitant every hour.

Mama and I took turns lying down. Mama slept a little. I lay down and shut my eyes when it was my turn, not expecting to sleep. I must have fallen asleep, though. Suddenly I was in the middle of a nightmare. Once again, Phrynion had invaded my home, Bardian's home, this house. Again, I was defenseless against the monster. He snapped a braided horsehide whip as he bent over me. I smelled his fetid breath. "The old whore and the young one, I've got you both now," he shouted in triumph.

"Mama!" I screamed. Before I could sit up, she was beside me, holding me, stroking my hair.

I told her my dream. "Perhaps this dream is sent as a warning," Mama said. She called one of the household slaves who slept outside our door. "Wake your mistress," she commanded. "Ask her to come at once."

"Is the old master dead?" The woman's eyes went at once to the bed.

"Not yet," Mama told her. "I need your mistress for a different reason."

Nerissa arrived more quickly than either of us expected, looking pale and anxious. "What has happened now?" she asked.

"If Phrynion tried to come into this house, would he be stopped at the gatehouse? More important, if he came with some of his men, *could* he be stopped?"

Nerissa gaped at us. "I don't know," she said at last. "He has been here so often. Sometimes I complained that he lived here more than in his own home. The gateman has always had orders to admit him at any hour. Whether Bardian left new orders or not, I've no idea. I don't talk to the gateman."

Mama looked at the fat woman in exasperation. "This is not practical at all," she said grimly. "Nerissa, come with me at once. Phano, you stay with Uncle Nikos."

I heard the ruckus at the gate, but even if there was

something to be seen from the balcony, I could not see it. No one got through into the courtyard. There was no motion, no sound in the dark space I watched. The fight, if it was a fight, was confined to the street. The temptation to run downstairs was terrible, but I conquered it. Grimly, I turned back to the bed. I'd know the worst soon enough.

We had given up trying to feed the dying man. I swabbed his mouth with cool water and changed the damp cloth on his forehead. Gently, I moistened his emaciated body with good olive oil.

Mama and Nerissa returned before I had finished. "The gates were shut," Mama reported, "but the keeper was groggy with sleep. Who knows what he would have done, if we had not arrived when we did? Bardian did not give direct orders when he and Stephanos drove off in such a hurry. He told the gateman to be careful, nothing more than that. We must be grateful to the god who sent your dream. When there's time, we'll make a proper sacrifice."

"Was it Phrynion at the gate?"

"I'm sure it was, though I've no proof. His voice was muffled, as if he spoke through a woolen scarf. He said he had a message from Bardian."

Nerissa looked livelier than I'd ever seen her. "Nera shouted that I was ready to hear his message, but I would not open the gate at night with the master away," she said. "That was quick thinking, Nera."

"When he heard that, there was some snarling and banging on the door," Mama said. "He had dogs with him as well as men. That's a good heavy door, though, and the bars held. He seemed to be very angry. I couldn't make out any words, but I could hear the rage."

"So could I." Nerissa shivered.

"Has the man lost his wits?" I was puzzled. "Are the Furies chasing him? The priestess warned him he would be watched. Does he believe it was an idle threat? He must know better."

"What can we do?" Nerissa wailed. "I need my husband. I need Bardian. I need him *now*."

"Whether the Furies are after him or not, Phrynion is dangerous," said Mama. I needed no reminder. Sometimes we speak of the Furies as the Kindly Ones, but that's because we are desperately afraid of the horrid creatures, all dressed in black with snaky hair and blood dripping from their eyes, sent to drive a sinner mad. If anyone deserved to have such creatures following at his heels, Phrynion was the man; yet I felt sick thinking of such a fate, even for Phrynion.

# twenty-four

Theo, Stephanos and Bardian arrived early the following day. We had summoned them, but Theo was quick to tell us that their work was done. The archons of Athens had hammered out changes to put teeth into our city's agreement with Thebes. Athens and Thebes would stand together against the threat from the north.

"Too little, too late," said Father, rubbing his tired eyes. "I'm too old for this."

"It's better than it was, by a long shot," said Theo. "Better yet, we Athenians aren't wasting more time and money bickering among ourselves: rich and poor have come to an agreement. You have helped to bring that about, Bardian. Well done, Uncle."

"You understand how it was, Theo. Phrynion convinced me that rich men like me could keep our money and our freedom too, and Athens would not suffer. We *wanted* to believe him, so we did; nothing easier. And after all I'd done for him, he threatened me. *Me!* Did he think I'd lie down and let myself be ruined?" Bardian sounded as obnoxious as ever. However, he was no longer angry at me and Theo. That was an improvement.

"Can Thebes and Athens together stand against Philip?" I asked.

"For the time being," said Father. "It won't last, of course. Everything changes." I stared from him to Mama and back again.

Mama's rich laughter filled the room. "I said as much to Phano only yesterday," she said. "Husband, you borrowed my very words! However, this alliance with Thebes is good. Your grandson will begin his life in a city at peace." After that statement, there was much oohing and aahing from those who hadn't known about my pregnancy. Nerissa should have been the person to cut it off, but she showed no sign of doing so; nor did Mama. Helen and Dora and Bouly's parents had been sent for, Bouly as well, but they had not yet arrived.

We were not in Uncle Nikos's sickroom, but in the great room of the women's quarters. I stood near the door. With a turn of my head, I could see the sickbed with its slight burden. Beyond, the balcony door was open to the sky.

"It's wonderful that all of you are happy about the

baby," I said, "granddaughter or grandson, Mama, as the gods decide. But we've plenty of time for that. We women called the family to take leave of Uncle Nikos and to make the arrangements for his funeral. Let's sit with him now and put other thoughts aside."

We sat by the bedside for an hour or so, as the light breathing grew lighter. At some point, a hand caressed my shoulders. I looked up, startled: Bouly! She took her place beside me. There was little space between mourners; nonetheless, it was a comfort to feel my friend's warm, solid body beside mine.

Twice Uncle Nikos stopped breathing, and Mama bent over the bed, but there was a little gasp and the sighing breaths resumed. Then they stopped for the third time. We all held our breath until we could hold it no longer, but Uncle Nikos did not breathe again. "He was a good man," said Mama gently. "Many will mourn for him."

The same women who had bathed me for my wedding bathed Uncle Nikos for his funeral. I had changed my role in the ceremony, of course, and we bathed the ravaged body on the bed, not in a tub, but somebody had added the same mix of herbs to the water; the air was heavy with the pungent scent of thyme.

Nerissa put a small coin on each eye to keep it shut. Bardian brought the ceremonial coins for the ferryman. We placed them under Uncle Nikos's tongue and bound up his jaw to keep his mouth closed. His ghost might be lingering nearby, but now it had no way to get back into his body.

While we worked, servants cleared the andron, where the men held their dinners, and set up a couch to receive the corpse. When we were ready, we would carry Uncle Nikos down. Nerissa left the rest of us to dress him in long black corpse clothes, while she went off to search for the crown.

She came back, whining, "I can't find Father's gilded crown of wild olive."

I have never met a less practical woman. Nerissa had no coins ready for Uncle's eyelids—Mama had had to provide them—and now she couldn't find the crown. Why hadn't she put everything together? Bardian was no help, of course; it's the wife's job. I stopped myself from glaring at the stupid woman.

My husband, always the diplomat, spoke kindly. "Was that his prize from the Great Festival when he was a boy?" Theo asked. "He showed it to me once."

"What contest did he win?" I asked. My anger had come and gone like a flash of lightning; Theo can always drain it quickly, perhaps because I love him. "Did your uncle want you to compete in it?"

"Not after he heard my voice." Theo chuckled. "He won the crown for singing to the harp. He was a famous singer when he was young. I'm sorry you never heard him."

"That crown is worth one thousand drachmas." Bardian's voice was sharp. "What's the matter with you, Nerissa? You should know exactly where it is."

"Come, Phano," said my husband. "You are good at finding everything. Let's help Nerissa."

Bardian's vaults were lined with great jars of precious olive oil, wine and grain, rows and rows of them. His treasure room was piled high with chests. So much wealth! It seemed to me that Bardian could build two or three triremes and never notice the cost. "This search could take all night," I said.

Luckily I was wrong. Theo and Nerissa identified three or four likely chests. The crown was in the second one, wrapped in fine linen. The gold-encrusted olive leaves glimmered in the light of our oil lamps. We took the precious bundle to the andron. Bardian chose to carry his father's body down, though the slight weight would have been easy for any one of us.

Bardian laid the old man on the couch. Nerissa settled the gold crown on his head. For two days he would lie here. All the important people of Athens would come to say farewell. With the crown in place, and the black clothes properly arranged, Uncle Nikos looked both peaceful and majestic. Servants brought baskets of early flowers and green branches for us to strew around him. I was glad we could all remember him like this.

"Will you bury the crown with him?" I asked Nerissa. I knew she would say yes; I was working my way toward asking something else.

"Of course," Nerissa replied.

"That's the right thing," Theo agreed. "It was his most valued possession."

Some of Mama's notions have certainly rubbed off on me. "When Athens needs triremes," I asked cautiously, "is it right to bury one thousand drachmas? Is that what

Uncle Nikos would want? He loved flowers. Wouldn't he be just as happy with a crown of delicate spring blooms?"

"How can you suggest such a thing!" Nerissa was shocked.

I shrugged. There was no point in making things difficult. "Of course you must do what seems right."

For the next two days, we women kept our places at Uncle Nikos's head. Often one or another of us would beat her head, or lift up her hands to the gods, or tear her hair. Sometimes women perform these actions of mourning, but anyone can see it's nothing but a performance. I believe all of us had cared for Uncle Nikos; our grief pervaded the room. For me, it was a relief to let my tears flow.

While other Athenians came to say farewell, we sang the ancient laments for the dead. Sometimes I broke down, weeping, but Dora's voice never faltered, though she had loved him far longer than I. My teacher did not come; she sent four priestesses, one of whom passed on her affectionate greeting to me.

Toward evening on the second day, a sudden silence fell. I was on my knees. I looked up, and there was Phrynion, standing at the foot of the couch, devouring me with his eyes. "Get out, goblin," I wanted to shout, but my mouth was dry. Phrynion stood there without moving. Like all the mourners, he was draped in black. His eyes were pools of blackness. His face was without expression.

We stared at each other forever, it seemed; then Theo

materialized at Phrynion's side. "Come with me," he said. "Thank you for coming to pay your respects in this house of mourning. Now it's time to leave."

What did it mean, that visit? That disgusting man left his evil scent on everything he touched, even my mourning. Theo's too. We puzzled over it that evening, while making sure that all was prepared for the final part in the ritual of death.

The cart waited in the courtyard. In the hours before dawn, Bardian again carried his father's body and laid it there. The men gathered behind him; then we women formed our procession behind Nerissa. Torchbearers stood ready. When the torches had been lighted, we set out. I had expected Uncle Nikos's body would be burned and the ashes collected in a funeral urn, but Theo told me his family usually buried their dead.

Bardian had hired mourners to sing and perform the old dances at the graveside. I looked around for Phrynion, half expecting him to wander into the light of a nearby torch, but he did not appear.

I had seen funerals many times, of course, but I had never been part of one before. Again and again, I was reminded of the rituals of my marriage. We carried fruit and nuts for our graveside offering, the same kind of shower that had welcomed me to my new home with Theo. Uncle Nikos's new home in the Underworld would not be in any way so pleasant. For this ceremony, as for my wedding, there would be a feast. We women watched and wailed while the body was lowered into the grave, but we left before the men to make sure the sweetmeats, bread and fruit were ready at home. I had walked with Dora, Helen and Mama behind Nerissa on the way to the burial place, but Bouly fell into place beside me and we talked quietly all the way back. It seems I will dance at Bouly's wedding after all.

※

"Will I always be looking over my shoulder for Phrynion?"

It was the day after the funeral, and I was home again. Dora and I sat comfortably together in the big upstairs room. For a wonder, I had no yarn in my hands. It felt as if I had been away for months, or years, though really it had been a matter of days, no more. Naturally, we talked of Phrynion's strange appearance at Uncle Nikos's funeral. Did Mother think he was mad?

"I never heard of the Furies chasing a monster," Dora said thoughtfully. "Criminals like Orestes or Oedipus, yes, or great Hercules himself, because of Hera's jealousy. You can't possibly feel sorry for Phrynion? Pregnancy does strange things, dear daughter, but that would be foolish of you. We'd do better to send word to the temple of Dionysos."

"No need to do that," I replied. "She knows."

"Her watchers could have missed it. You should send word. It was a shock to you, seeing him there. Weren't you looking over your shoulder at the burying last night? I was.

We don't want to live that way, always wondering what he's plotting and when he may appear."

"I don't even want to think about Phrynion, let alone see him," I burst out. "All right, Mother, I will send a messenger."

However, the message was never sent. Delia, Phrynion's housekeeper, who taught me to spin, arrived while Dora and I were still talking. She had come to tell us her master had disappeared in the night. His horses and his treasure chest were gone as well.

"He gave me no warning," she said, "but then I wouldn't expect it. He has always treated me as a slave, though I am not."

"Phrynion treats all his servants like slaves," I said. "I'm surprised you dared to come here, Delia."

"Me too," said Delia, "but I don't think he will be back for some time. No doubt he'll send for his heavy goods, and for his household servants."

"Will you go?"

"What else? I have served his family all my life. He treated you unkindly as a child, Basilinna; sometimes I still have bad dreams about the scrawny mite with the big dark eyes who sat beside me and learned to spin. I showed you how to hold your spindle, how to load your distaff."

"You were my first weaving teacher too, Delia."

"And Phrynion seized the blanket you made. So much work for a child's fingers! He told me to sell it in the marketplace, but I gave him the value of it myself and hid it away. That's why I came today, to bring it to you." She took it from her bag and handed it to me. "Someday you may give it to your daughter," she said.

A little thing can make me cry these days, but this was no little thing. My first blanket!—a child's work, full of knots, but even more full of memories, and not all of them were bad. I buried my face in it and wept.

Bardian's first announcement as new head of the family was to pledge not only one but two triremes, fully equipped, complete with crews, for the defense of Athens and her partner Thebes. It was more than a pledge. Shipwrights began work on the first vessel immediately. Coming on the heels of this announcement, Phrynion's conviction for treacherous dealing with Macedon had no visible impact on Theo's family. No doubt it's easier to convict when the accused person is absent, but by all reports the evidence was overwhelming. Phrynion probably was warned. We were thankful he had done nothing in public to discredit Bardian.

"Brilliant idea about the triremes," I told Theo when at last we had a little time to ourselves. "Who thought of it, you or Bardian?" My husband did not reply.

"Father? Was it Father?" I took a feather and tickled Theo's feet. "Tell me, tell me." We both dissolved in giggles. Theo tickled my belly, and we giggled some more. I *liked* pretending to be a child again. I liked being happy, carefree and pregnant. I had been serious for too long.

"We all got the idea about the same time," said Theo, "but honestly, I think Stephanos said it first. He mentioned only one ship, however; the second one was my inspiration.

"The big surprise was our cousin. I expected Bardian to go along with us. I couldn't think of any other way for him to separate himself publicly from Phrynion. I did not expect him to be thrilled about so costly a solution, but he was as pleased as I've ever seen him. Maybe he always wanted honor more than money; he just didn't know it. He set a splendid example. All the other rich families had to come forward. Ten more ships are being built, and every mason in Attica is cutting stone or rebuilding the damaged sections of the Long Walls. The treasury of Athens is filled to bursting. Thebes is hiring mercenaries, and we'll pay them, since we don't have much of an army. If Philip thought he was going to march into our country and take over, he knows better now."

Since the end of Theo's term of office, we have lived very quietly. We've heard no whisper of Phrynion, and we do not know where he has gone. He won't find an easy welcome anywhere, it seems to me. Theo believes he has gone to Macedon, and that soon we'll hear of him serving Philip openly.

I doubt this. Phrynion does not thrive in the open; he does his work in the dark. Someday someone will roll aside a large rock and he'll crawl out. Or not. It is possible that the high priestess of Dionysos judged him and acted to silence him. If so, she probably would not inform me. It would be a dangerous secret, a burden as well as a relief. I won't feel really safe until I know the beast is dead, and I may never know with certainty. However, Phrynion seldom invades my dreams.

My belly walks in front of me these days. The nights are long; in the morning, the courtyard is white with frost. Soon my baby will be born. Everything is ready, though I continue to spin fine yarn and to weave cloth like gossamer. No prince could be better clothed than my baby will be. Forgive me, great Athene, I never meant to sound so proud.

Helen has given me a new thigh shield, the mate to my old one, except that the birds on it are geese, not partridges. That was a surprise: my dear old thigh shield had a twin. I say "Grandmother" to her when I think of it, because it pleases her, but it doesn't come without thinking. When she's truly a great-grandmother, it will be easier.

Speaking of geese, Newby brought a procession of goslings into the courtyard yesterday. Nothing would content her until I marched around in front of her. She followed me proudly, and her brood followed her. Dora laughed until she cried. In Newby's eyes, I am a grandmother!

I must make sure that Newby hatches a chick about the time my own son or daughter begins to toddle. For the present, Athens is as safe as Theo and I could make her, but it's only right that our little one should have his—or her—very own special guard.

# afterword

The idea for this novel came from a prosecutor's speech delivered before an Athenian jury between 343 and 340 B.C.E., several years after the events in my book. The outcome of the trial is unknown—indeed, nothing about it has survived except the prosecutor's address. Even that has probably been preserved because of a mistake: for centuries the speech was wrongly attributed to the famous orator Demosthenes. Modern scholars now believe that the speech was delivered by Apollodoros, a much less important figure.

From this speech, it is clear that an aging courtesan named Neaira was prosecuted because she had allegedly broken the law that forbade foreigners to marry or pretend lawful marriage with an Athenian citizen. (*Foreigner* or *metic* meant anybody who was neither a citizen nor a slave, not necessarily a person who came from somewhere else.) Neaira was also accused of illegally marrying her daughter, Phano, to an Athenian citizen, an archon.

This prosecution was political rather than personal. If it succeeded, Neaira's husband, Stephanos, would have been ruined by a heavy fine, a pointed message for like-minded politicians. He was the real target in the proceedings. However, if the case went against her, Neaira would have been sold into slavery. The man behind the prosecution may well have been Phrynion, whose enmity fueled more than one vicious attack on Stephanos and Neaira.

History is constantly being reevaluated, sometimes in the light of new discoveries but often as a result of new ways of looking at the same old facts. For most scholars, until the most recent times, the mud flung in the prosecutor's speech has stuck. He said that Stephanos was a black-mailer and a cheat, and that Neaira was a prostitute and so was her daughter, Phano, whom she had fraudulently married to Theogenes. As Basilinna, Phano had profaned the Mysteries and exposed Athens to danger from angry gods. Further, by posing as a citizen, she had endangered all the wives and daughters of Athens.

Was it so?

Almost certainly it was not. The prosecutor's objective was to inflame the jury (a large jury, consisting of one hundred, two hundred, or even three hundred men). He said less about Phano than he would certainly have done if his charge had been true, though he used slander and innuendo that outrage us today. However, Athenian citizen families did not enter lightly into a marriage. The family of Theogenes would have checked Phano's antecedents thoroughly—just as, in my novel, his mother says they did. From this premise, it follows that Phano was not Neaira's daughter; as the daughter of a courtesan who had been a slave, she would not have been acceptable.

Athens is famous as the cradle of democracy; however, this was not democracy as we understand it. Important state positions were filled by election, but those eligible to vote and to hold office consisted of a fairly small group of citizen men.

In another way, ancient Athens was very different from our society today. The culture was based on slavery. By 350 B.C.E., slavery had become institutionalized. Slaves were born to other slaves or sold into slavery by poor, noncitizen parents. They had few rights; they were not regarded as fully functional persons. No doubt some owners treated their slaves with trust and respect, but many were abused, with virtually no recourse.

Slavery is not the only aspect of life in ancient Athens likely to shock a modern reader. Women and children had little independence or authority. Economically, socially and sexually, their lives were controlled by men, in law if not always in practice.

Perhaps the culture was more repressive because of the growing threat from the north. By 350 B.C.E., King Philip II of Macedon was only twelve years away from crushing Athens and Thebes at the battle of Chaeronea, forever ending Athens's days as a major military and naval power.

Much of ancient Athens belongs to the unknowable past. Then, as now, the normal and uneventful were usually not recorded. I have used what scholarship offers, and built on it. Athenian culture then was certainly different from today; but the feelings of the people weren't all that different, and they worked out their hopes and dreams in ways that resonate with modern readers.

# ❀ acknowledgments ❀

Writing a historical novel with a setting so ancient is like putting together a puzzle. I've found pieces in Toronto, Britain and Greece, in libraries, on the Internet and in museums and tombs, among them the tomb of King Philip himself in northern Greece. I've gathered evidence not only from books and maps but from people as well, ranging from consular staff to classical scholars.

I've been obsessed with these people and their story. When focused to this extent, I set out to find out everything about the people, the time, the place, the culture. Then serendipity takes over. Who would have thought that my agents, Lynn and David Bennett, would offer my husband and me a month's stay at their cottage in Toot Baldon, twelve miles from Oxford's Bodleian Library and Ashmolean Museum and its library, two of the finest resources in the world for my research? Who would have dreamed that my granddaughter Leigh Halliwell-Beck and her family would move to Greece, and that Leigh would drive my husband and me to visit King Philip's tomb? Naturally, Vicki Megas and George Hadzichrisostomou, friends of a friend, drove us to spend a magical weekend at their holiday home in Halkidiki and demonstrated unforgettably that traditions of Greek hospitality have not declined in twenty-five hundred years.

Dr. Peter Baiter, Director, Pinewood International School of Thessaloníki, provided useful advice about dealing with Greek names in a modern English novel. Museum staff and curators in Thessaloníki, Athens and Crete did their best to answer my many questions. Other major sources have been the University of Toronto's Robarts Library, where I began my research, and the Internet; I pay special tribute to the Perseus Digital Library on Ancient Greece (www.perseus.tufts.edu). Mary R. Lefkowitz and Maureen B. Fant first brought Neaera's story (their spelling) to my attention in their excellent 1977 volume, *Women in Greece and Rome*, which contains a lengthy excerpt from the speech, still attributed to Demosthenes, who became a character in early versions of my book. That had to change when I found Peter Carey's 1992 translation and notes, though Carey's disapproving view of the characters echoed that of Apollodoros. Then, in Oxford, Konstantinos Kapparis's 1999 translation and notes appeared. Here was a scholar who agreed with my conclusion that the prosecutor's speech was unlikely to provide an unbiased view of Neaira or her family.

My editor at Delacorte Press, Karen Wojtyla, has made many useful suggestions, carefully and tentatively proffered; she has shared my excitement about the manuscript, and has worked with me through some difficult changes. Thanks to peerless copy editor Barbara Perris, also at Delacorte Press. Thanks to Margaret Atwood for her gracious permission to use the epigraph from *The Blind Assassin*. Members of my writing group have been the first audience for my works in progress for twenty years: Sylvia Warsh, Heather Kirk, Vancy Kasper, Lorraine Williams, Barbara Kerslake and Ayanna Black. My husband, Howard Collum, has given me the greatest gift any partner can give to a writer: supporting my rhythms and needs, whether understanding that I had to get up if my characters began talking to me in the middle of the night, or making his splendid grilled cheese sandwiches for dinner when I had spent the day at my computer and was too tired to think, let alone cook. Thank you, all.

# ✻ glossary ✻

AGORA: A meeting place, marketplace; in ancient Athens, a large (about the size of three football fields) central open space where citizens gathered to get the daily news and to engage in important state activities, commercial, political and judicial. Although open, the agora was not bare; trees and small shrines gave it a parklike ambience.

ANDRON: A room for men's banquets in an ancient Greek house.

ANTHESTERIA: A festival of wine and of spirits from the unseen world, with a focus on the sacred marriage of the Basilinna to Dionysos, the god of wine. In Athens, the three-day celebration began on the eleventh day of Anthesterion.
> Day 1—Day of the Jars: Enormous jars of new wine, pressed the previous fall, were opened and sampled.
> Day 2—Day of the Jugs: Everybody had a small jug for sampling; these jugs had a distinct big-bellied shape. This was Phano's great day, a day of sacrifice to Dionysos and the Basilinna's ritual marriage to the god.
> Day 3—Day of the Pots: Food for the dead was boiled in special pots, and sacrifices were offered to placate vengeful spirits.

ANTHESTERION: One of twelve lunar months in the Athenian calendar, starting roughly at the end of February.

APATURIA: An autumn festival, when young children were introduced to their clans. In Phano's Athens, one festival followed another, often only a few days later. Another autumn festival was Oschophoria.

ARCHON: One of the nine rulers or principal magistrates of ancient Athens, chosen by lot.

AREOPAGOS: The prime council of Athens.

BASILEUS: The King Archon, one of the nine ruling magistrates.

BASILINNA: The wife of the Basileus.

FEMALE CLOTHING—E.G., CHITON, PEPLOS, HIMATION:

The *PEPLOS* was a draped tunic made from a single rectangle of woolen fabric joined at each shoulder with one long pin; it gave way to the chiton about the sixth century B.C.

The *CHITON* was also made from a single rectangle, but its fabric was lighter and much wider than that used for the peplos, measuring up to ten feet wide. The enormous width required five to ten fibulae (brooches) to fasten the top edge, leaving an openwork seam on each side of the neck that ran across the shoulders and down the arms to form elbow-length sleeves.

The *HIMATION*, usually worn over a chiton, was a flowing garment gathered around a woman's arms, sometimes covering her shoulders; a fold of it doubled as a head covering or veil.

Men also wore chitons and himations, but the style was different from women's garments. To avoid confusion, I've used *tunic* and *cloak* for men's clothes.

HETAIRA: A courtesan or concubine in ancient Greece; a specially trained, educated female companion. *Courtesan* is the nearest English word in common use, though it is not an exact equivalent.

MONEY: 6 obols = 1 drachma, 100 drachmas = 1 mina, 60 minas = 1 talent.

Monetary values in ancient Greece were variable, and surviving records are woefully incomplete. Stephanos's little house in Athens was said to be worth 7,000 drachmas; Phano's dowry was 6,000 drachmas, while Phrynion's gift (or loan) was 15 minas, or 1,500 drachmas, half the value of a high-priced slave.

OLIGARCHY: Government by a few, usually like-minded, people.

PEDAGOGOS: A slave who supervised children, usually taking them to and from school.

PHILIPPEIOI: Coins minted by King Philip II, ruler of Macedon from 359 to 336 B.C.E. and father of Alexander the Great.

POLEMARCH: An archon who dealt with legal matters involving foreigners (noncitizens).

TRIREME: A fighting ship designed to cover long distances quickly under oar and sail, and in battle to ram enemy ships with devastating effect. A trireme was 121 feet long, with an 18-foot beam, rowed by 170 men in three tiers on each side, one man to an oar. Oars in the tiers were either 13 feet, 8 inches long or 13 feet long; shorter oars were used at the bow and stern. The large square sail was left ashore when the ship prepared for battle. In her glory days, Athens dominated the Mediterranean by means of her fleet of triremes.

# ❊ about the author ❊

PRISCILLA GALLOWAY is the author of *Truly Grim Tales*, an ALA Best Book for Young Adults, and *Snake Dreamer*, which *School Library Journal* called "a thought-provoking meeting of myth and modern science." Her non-fiction work *Too Young to Fight: Memories from Our Youth During World War II* won the Bologna Ragazzi Award for Young Adult Nonfiction.

Priscilla Galloway has taught in high schools and universities and has been honored as Teacher of the Year by the Ontario Council of Teachers of English. Born in Montreal, she has lived, written, taught and scuba dived from the Pacific to the Atlantic, from the southern farming country to the northern mines, from the Caribbean to New Zealand. Her home base is Toronto.